EVE LANGLAIS

1

I BECAME A PARIAH A FEW MONTHS BEFORE
graduation—less than six before my eighteenth
birthday.

With one video uploaded to the internet, my life
was ruined. And not because of anything I did.

The cops managed to make it to my school
before social media ran wild with the news, which
was surprising in this day and age.

In those moments before my world crumbled, I
doodled on my laptop mousepad as the teacher
droned on and on. My note-taking program allowed
me to freehand, so I slid my finger on the smooth,
gray square, swirling outlines of hearts that I filled in.
I dragged lightning bolts to bisect them. No initials,
though. I learned my lesson in my grade-ten biology
class, when Hayley snapped a pic over my shoulder

and posted it online for everyone to see. The next day, when I sat down in my English class, the kids began singing, *"Abigail and Connor, sitting in a tree..."*

It was a wonder I didn't die. The object of my crush did his best to pretend I didn't exist. Unless he got me alone, then he had all kinds of ideas about the things we could do. I declined. The reality of him proved much less attractive than my fantasy.

Sadly, that seemed to be a running theme.

At a knock, the teacher—Mr. Godfrey, who always wore a sweater, even if we were sweating because the air-conditioning was broken again—paused in his lecture to answer it, sticking his head out the door. A murmur of voices sounded, and Mr. Godfrey slipped fully into the hall to deal with it. The door closed, and the class erupted into noise, not so much talking as reaching for phones. As if the students were drones with a hive mind, the classroom filled with the hum of music and voices leaking from earbuds as videos and games were played. At times like these, when all the heads were bent and intent over screens, an eerie unease filled me.

Unnatural. In the movies—the old ones that showed a classroom setting—people talked. Joked around. Flirted. Now, we did a lot of that online. Looking for likes. Wanting to go viral.

My mom called it an addiction, and after being bullied a few times online, she'd forced me off all of it. My cell phone didn't have internet capabilities. Just plain talk and text. Which was why it stayed in my bag. After all, who would I message?

I was the new kid again. I'd arrived at the beginning of my senior year. I hadn't bothered to make many friends because I knew I'd be leaving for college. Even if I weren't, my parents never stayed in one place for long.

Slouched in my seat and bored, I drummed my fingers, waiting to get out of class. I'd already aced this course. Calculus. A math I'd probably never use again. What I needed was to study for an exam next week in chemistry. A ninety on it would help cement my A in that class.

Yes, I was a nerd. The kind with a book at home that I'd stayed up a little too late reading. My eyes burned this morning. Blame the fatigue for not realizing that Mr. Godfrey had called my name.

"Abigail Smith. Could you come here, please?" the teacher said firmly and, judging by the chuckles in the class, it wasn't the first time.

My cheeks heated as I lifted my gaze to Mr. Godfrey and noticed he stood beside a pair of police officers.

"Yes, Mr. Godfrey. Sorry."

Rather than reply, he beckoned, and with great reluctance, I rose from my seat, knowing everybody watched. It made my movements jerky. My hip hit my desk, and as the metal leg dragged, it made a horrible screeching noise that drew a titter. Being the center of attention made me want to sink into the floor.

Don't look at me.

I ducked my head for the walk of burning shame. My cheeks were hot as I endured the titters, the stares, the judgement.

What possible reason could there be for me to talk to the cops? I'd just refuse. They couldn't question me without my mom's and dad's permission. It hit me then.

There was only one reason for the police to pull me out of class.

This had to be really bad. Oh, my fucking God. My parents had an accident.

Had to be. Why else would they be here asking for me?

I didn't do drugs. Never got in fights. I was boring and perfect. Just what I needed to get into any college I wanted. I had three acceptances already—two of them with small scholarships.

As I neared the police officers, I took note of their appearance. The pair of them were grim-faced. The

4

older one was jowly cheeked, and his belly bulged over his pants. His ill-fitting coat didn't quite hide the harness with the gun in it. His partner was a much shorter woman with blond hair cut short, her figure trim. She had her hand on the weapon by her side.

I swallowed hard. "Hi, I'm Abby." Probably the stupidest thing in the world I could have said.

Stu-pid-est.

"We need you to come with us," the older cop said.

"Why?" I thought it was a simple question, but the short one snapped, "Don't talk back. We're here about your parents."

The horrible feeling in my stomach exploded. "Oh my God, they're dead, aren't they? Oh, no." Tears rushed to my eyes, and I could see the horror in their dropped jaws and wide gazes. It only confirmed the fact that I was all alone.

In my grief, it took a moment for words to penetrate. Mr. Godfrey tried to explain my very faulty reasoning. "Your parents aren't dead. This is much worse."

How could it be worse? Later on, I understood the why, but in the moment, elation filled me that my parents lived. "How badly were they injured? Can I go see them?"

The bigger cop leaned into me, and I smelled cigarettes under the minty gum he chewed. "Do you know where they are?"

I frowned. "If they're not in the hospital, then they should be at work."

"They're not there," the woman cop said. "Where else could they be?"

"I don't know. Have you tried calling them?"

"Could you call them for us?"

"Why me? The school has their number."

"Just do it," snapped the female cop, still with a hand on her gun. Would she really shoot me?

"My phone is in my bag."

"Go get it!"

How was it I didn't die? Surely, the embarrassment should have killed me. Head ducked, I walk back to my desk, bent to get my bag, fumbled with my phone, all the while sweating because...geezus, the cop lady was actually pulling her gun.

I waved my phone as I headed back towards the classroom door. "Found it. Want me to call them now?"

"Yes," the older cop stated and put a hand on his partner's arm.

Number one on my speed dial. It rang and rang. Went to voicemail. No big deal. They were probably at work.

"Call again."

As I redialed, I eyed their serious miens. "Why are you looking for my parents?"

When all the adults shared a look, my stomach seized, knotting into a tight ball. "What is going on?"

It was Jarrod, who never paid attention to anything but his phone during class, who shouted, "Holy shit! There's a manhunt on for Abby's parents. They're the Pentagram Killers."

2

No FEELING CAN COMPARE TO FINDING OUT your parents are serial killers. And not just suspected, I should add. My parents were honest-to-God, caught-on-camera killers. The fancy kind that created great big ol' pentagrams as a stage for murder.

I'd heard of them, the Pentagram Killers. Everyone had. They'd been all over the internet since the documentary came out. Apparently, someone had noticed a trend in crimes spanning more than a dozen states and going back about eighteen years. People had theories about those murders because they were quite extraordinary. While it was clear that someone had died, no bodies were ever found.

After that report came out, a pentagram had

been found in my town. Same *modus operandi* or MO—the fancy term everyone used since that crime scene was similar to those in the documentary. Made scarier by the fact that the cops had no real suspects. Knowing a killer might be in their midst brought out the fear in the residents. Neighbors eyed each other suspiciously. Calls to emergency increased as everything got overly scrutinized.

Even with my internet blackout, I'd heard about it and asked my parents. They'd shrugged and said not to worry about it. Probably just someone copycatting because of the miniseries.

We dropped the subject because Mom suddenly asked, "Did you decide on a college yet? We really should get packing for a move."

"Is Abigail a killer, too?" The high-pitched, giddy exclamation had me turning cold and snapped me back to the present.

"No. It's not true." This had to be a nightmare. Only I could see by the faces of the adults eyeing me that it wasn't.

Shock set in, making me a malleable doll who followed the police down the hall and out of the school to the police car sitting near the curb. I halted. This couldn't be real.

"Keep moving." The barked command jostled free my voice.

"No. You aren't allowed to take me." I knew my rights. Kind of. "I want my parents."

"So do we," was the snarky reply.

"Are you just going to let them take me?" I asked in desperation as I glanced at the principal and the other teaching staff watching. None of them stepped in. No one said a word. Surely, this wasn't legal.

"I'm sure you'll be fine," was the principal's halting reply.

"Fine?" An incredulous rejoinder that led to the cop losing patience.

"Let's go."

"Go where?"

"The police station."

The nightmare thickened. "Am I being arrested?"

"Given the situation, you're being taken into custody for your own safety." A hand on my elbow jerked me forward, and I stumbled.

"I'm not in any danger, though. Whatever you think my parents did, you're wrong."

"Don't fight, or this will get much harder," the older cop interjected, his tone weary.

But I wanted to fight and scream. This couldn't be happening.

I got into the back seat of the police car, simmering at the unfairness. I'd committed no crime.

How dare they treat me so unjustly? My parents would be so mad when they found out. Because whatever the rumor floating around on the internet, it couldn't be true. My parents weren't killers.

The two cops didn't show me any softness as they ordered me to accompany them into the police station. We had to brave a crowd holding up their phones, screaming questions.

"Is that the daughter?"

"Does she know where her parents are?"

"Did she help them?"

The very idea had me sinking deeply into myself. What'd happened to my morning? It'd begun so well, too, with a new box of my favorite cereal—pure crunchy, sweet, sugary deliciousness. As I ate, my mom had told me there used to be toys inside the box when she was young. Whereupon, I'd argued. Why would a company need to bribe children to eat? Shouldn't the food be good on its own?

Shock swept me past the mob of faces and into the police station. I'd never been inside one before. But I wasn't given time to stand around and gawk. The cops ushered me into a room, the walls white with scuffs all over. The table was metal and bolted to the floor. The chair also fixed in place.

The officers left me alone but didn't take my phone. I couldn't decide if that was good or bad. I was a mess of nerves. What would happen to me? I just wanted my mom and dad.

How long could they keep me here?

I really had to pee.

Didn't feel well either. The room felt too small. Confining. Without even a window. Did it have enough air? It felt thin. I panted and sweated. Felt worse and worse. My stomach heaved, and with nowhere to throw up but the floor, I leaned over and spewed my not-so-sweet-now cereal.

Which was when the cop came in.

3

I DIDN'T MAKE A GREAT FIRST IMPRESSION. Neither did the cop with his gut hanging over his pants, given he exclaimed, "Geezus fucking Christ on a stick. Someone call fucking maintenance. We got a puker." The officer skirted the mess and slammed a binder onto the table.

I jumped.

"I'm detective Olsen. You're Abigail Smith, daughter of Lily and Geoffrey Smith."

"I want my phone call." According to television shows and movies, it was my right to demand one.

"You're not under arrest. And someone has already been contacted about you."

"Oh? Who? Did you find my parents?" I couldn't help a hopeful note.

"I ask the questions here," Olsen barked.

The situation overwhelmed, and I began to cry. Big snot bubbles and tears, which led to an exasperated, "For fuck's sake, pull yourself together."

"I d-d-d-on't un-un-underst-stand." I stammered my way through the words.

He uttered a bold, "We have evidence that your parents are the Pentagram Killers."

"No." I shook my head. "They're not." Not the woman who tucked me in every night with a kiss. Or the man who drove me to school every morning and said, "Knock 'em dead, Abby girl."

Out came the cop's phone. As he swiped, I took note of his thinning, short gray hair and angular frame. He smelled of cigarette smoke. He set his phone on the table between us and zoomed in on a face. "Know this guy?"

"No." The man with dark hair and plain features didn't spark anything.

"Are you sure?"

I shrugged. "Sorry."

"What about these people?" He pulled up two more images: a wide-eyed woman, and a man with his mouth open as if he were yelling something.

I gasped. "Those're my parents."

"Are you sure?"

It was only then I wondered if he'd set a trap for me. Why would he be so adamant? "Why are you asking? Who was that man in the first picture?"

"The victim your parents murdered." He sneered it, as if it were a fact.

The assertion angered. "Says who? I know my mom and dad. They wouldn't murder anyone." Dad was the kind to rescue spiders and put them outside.

"Really? Then maybe you can explain this." He loaded a video next.

A gruesome thing, the only saving grace being that it began after the murder, when the blood ran slick and wet. All kinds of disturbing shit happened in the clip. Maybe that's why I couldn't help hitting replay over and over.

Trying to make sense of it.

The video was of a room with walls made of concrete block, no insulation, nothing to soften the stark appearance. The area being filmed didn't contain any kind of furniture or detritus, probably due to the sump pump in the far corner, and the demarcation line on the walls. Valley areas tended to get hit often by the spring floods, but come summer, there wasn't any nicer land. So, owners tolerated their basements getting wet.

The illumination came from candles. Bright red ones, fat and solid, those that didn't require a holder to stand—one on each point of a pentagram. A few more were scattered around the room, causing light and shadow to flicker.

It appeared like a scene from a horror movie. I should know. I'd watched more than my fair share.

The video began shakily, first showing the steps going down, then the concrete floor before panning upwards, a slow-motion slide that brought into relief the blood pooling in the pentagram, spilled from a shape outside of it. Or so the video implied, given the body didn't move.

Freaky to see. But not the focal point of the video, I realized, as people in robes etched with symbols that shimmered when they moved came into view. A male voice chanted, and one of the shapes knelt and placed their hands in the pooling blood.

The other robed figure stood silently behind as the chant increased in tempo, and the blood appeared to steam and bubble.

A noise, a movement—who knew what it was—drew attention. The robed pair turned to face the person with the camera, the visages within the cowls dark pits.

One of them lunged for the person filming, and I heard my mom's voice. "Don't let them get away."

And then my dad's. "Hand that over."

The cops wouldn't know my parents' voices, which meant I dreaded what came next, recalling the pictures Olsen had shown me. The video took a turn. My father grappled with the person holding the camera, and it fell. It kept recording as they tussled. A hood was drawn back, and my father's face appeared.

Clean-shaven as of a few weeks ago because I'd complained that his beard and mustache were prickly. I never told him I missed them. His expression was fierce, rigid, and his eyes caught the light, glowing almost red.

The video stopped as a foot came down on the phone.

I threw up again, only nothing came up this time but painful heaves.

"Do you know those people in the video?"

"N-n-no." I denied it because it couldn't be real.

"Liar!" he barked.

Through tears and snot, I wailed. "No. It's fake."

As he opened his mouth to yell some more, the door to the room opened, and another cop entered. I heard the officer whispering to Olsen. Something about needing to wait and follow the rules so anything I said didn't get tossed.

But Olsen wouldn't be deterred. "Fuck the bureaucratic nonsense. This is a murder investigation. We can't afford to wait." He turned his mean gaze on me. "Where are your parents?"

"I d-d-don't know." The honest-to-God truth. Because if I knew, I'd call them and have them end this horrific nightmare.

"Tell me! Why would you protect monsters?" He slammed the phone back in front of me. The video began to play.

After the fourth time, the cop took back his cell and drawled, "Still going to deny your parents are the Pentagram Killers?"

"I—" I wanted to tell Olsen to go to Hell. I wanted to cry. Puke. Most of all, I wanted my mom and dad to hug me.

Instead, I got a social worker who slammed into the room and snapped, "This interview is over."

4

"It's over when I say it's over," Olsen snarled, rising to the occasion.

"You're questioning a minor without a guardian," the social worker said. Her hair was the kind of blond that needed help from a bottle.

"Not much choice given we're trying to locate her parents," Olsen argued.

"Speaking of choice, what kind of bad idea has a grown man in a room alone with a young girl, using his position of authority and his toxic masculinity to browbeat her?"

"I never touched her or said nothing!" Olsen huffed, suddenly defensive. "It's being recorded."

"Says you," spat my new hero. "This is inappropriate, and it stops now."

"We need to find her parents. This is a matter of life and death."

"You know the rules."

"For fuck's sake, we just need to talk to her. She's not being charged," blustered Olsen.

The woman eyed me. "Do you know where your parents are?"

I shook my head.

"There you go. Find someone else to question. We're leaving."

I rose from my chair and grabbed my bag, only to have Olsen hold out his hand. "We'll need your phone and computer."

"But they're mine." I hugged my bag.

My social worker added, "Get a warrant."

As if those were magical words, Olsen held out a sheaf of papers with a triumphant grin. "Got it right here. Hand it over."

I relinquished my phone and laptop. There went my only link to the world. To my mom and dad. How would they call me?

"What's the password to get in?" he immediately asked as he turned on my cell.

"She doesn't have to answer that. We're done here. Let's go, Abigail." She exited the room, and I followed the social worker who'd yet to introduce herself.

"The nerve of them," she muttered as she led me out of the police station, through a side entrance apparently used for more delicate cases involving kids or abuse. Would have been nice if they'd brought me in that way.

"Sit in the front," she said when I paused by the side of the car. "I'm Cassidy, by the way. Sorry I didn't get here quicker. I got caught in traffic."

"What's going to happen to me?"

"That kind of depends on your parents."

"Detective Olsen said they're looking for them."

"Do you know where they are?" Cassidy asked.

"No." Even if I did, I'd never rat them out.

"If they do contact you, Abigail, you need to tell someone right away." Her worried glance told me what she thought.

My chin jutted in defiance. "My parents aren't the Pentagram Killers."

Again, Cassidy paused before saying, "My understanding is they have quite a bit of evidence."

"That video is a fake." I wrung my hands in my lap.

"I can't speak on that, but I will note that they had no right to speak to you without a guardian or legal counsel present."

"Doesn't matter how many times they ask. I don't know anything."

"Be that as it may, law enforcement will still insist on speaking with you."

Dread knotted my stomach. "When?"

"Once a lawyer is assigned. They'll arrange an appointment. Probably in the morning."

"Where am I sleeping tonight?" I really wanted to go home.

"We had to scramble to find a spot in the city. We had no fosters accepting kids your age, but there is a group home with a spare bed."

That sounded horrifying. "Can't I go to a friend's house?" I didn't have any family nearby. No grandparents or aunts and uncles. And, technically, I only had one kind-of friend. She'd been the new girl, too, and we'd hung out until she got a boyfriend.

"You're underage, Abigail, which means the state has to care for you until a guardian is found."

"Or my parents are proven innocent."

"Until that happens, you will be put in the care of someone responsible." Cassidy parked in front of a townhome that screamed: *lived-in*. The kid vaping on the stoop added an element of class. "Listen, Abigail. My file on you says you're seventeen, right?"

"Yeah."

"You only need to go where the state tells you until you turn eighteen."

"That's still months away," I exclaimed.

"Barely any time," she said, nodding and smiling as if I had agreed.

"I want to go home," I huffed, panic welling inside me. "I want my bed. My pillow. My pajamas."

"I'm sure we can get you some clothes."

As if I'd settle for scraps. "I want to go home."

"That's not possible. Let's go inside."

It meant brushing past the kid vaping, who said nothing, just eyeballed us. I wanted to run away, screaming. Instead, I remained quietly tucked behind Cassidy as a wide woman pulled open the door, her hair falling out of a messy bun.

"Hey, Joleene." Cassidy waved. "I've got a temporary for you."

Joleene took one look at me and shook her head. "Oh, hell no you don't, Cassidy. You ain't putting Slaughter Daughter in my house."

The term caught my attention.

"She's harmless," Cassidy declared.

"Says you. How do we know she's not a killer?"

The attack on my character had me huffing. "I would never hurt anyone."

Joleene scowled. "But your parents would, and they haven't been caught yet."

"It probably won't be long." Cassidy's statement lacked confidence.

"What if they come here looking for her? What

if they kill me and all the children in our beds? No. I won't do it." Joleene shook her head vehemently, hard enough that her sloppy bun listed fully to the side.

"I've got nowhere else to put her," Cassidy pled.

"If she's so harmless, put her on your own damned couch." Joleene went back inside, slamming the door.

Cassidy sighed.

The kid on the steps looked right at me, eyed me up and down, and sneered. "She's no killer."

Nope, and yet the name Slaughter Daughter stuck.

5

CASSIDY BUNDLED ME BACK INTO HER CAR AND made some calls. The answer was the same each time. No, they wouldn't take me. Was Cassidy smoking crack?

During it all, I withdrew, sinking deeper and deeper into myself.

I wasn't sure how long it was before Cassidy finally pulled over and showed me a sign of humanity by hugging me and murmuring, "Don't cry. We'll figure something out."

I was done with it, though. I...freaked. Like utterly lost my shit. I screamed about it being unfair. Cried. Made demands. And when that didn't get me home, I threatened.

Which was why Cassidy ended up taking me to the hospital, telling them I'd had a mental break, threatened to harm myself, and needed observation. They placed me in a locked room by myself.

For seventy-two hours.

Not that I remembered much of the first twenty-four. Whatever pill they gave me lulled me to sleep, where I dreamed. Imagined my dad came to see me and told me everything would be okay. Said to be strong.

When I woke, I did a lot of crying at first, which led to the hospital staff threatening more sedation. So, I swallowed my anguish and instead became angry. How dare they lock me up? Why had no one come for me? Surely my parents had fixed the misunderstanding by now. By the end of my seventy-two hours, I'd reached a tenuous peace. It proved to be my last calm moment for a while.

Part of me spent that time expecting my parents to come to my rescue and tell me it was all a giant mistake. The only people I saw were the doctors, Cassidy, and the cop stationed outside my door.

Apparently, I merited police protection. To keep me safe or everyone else?

I met my lawyer on the third day. Garrett Browning. I immediately crushed on him. Tall, dark, and handsome in a suit. He sprang me from the mental ward and gave me clothes, a can of cola, and a bag of chips.

"Thanks," I said after we'd escaped, me feeling a bit more human in my jeans and shoes. Cassidy must have gotten my stuff for me.

"Don't thank me yet. Because I'm late to the game, we won't have a chance to really chat before your interview with the police." He led me through a maze of halls to the main level.

"I don't know anything."

"You don't have to lie to me," he stated. "As your lawyer, I'm on your side. But I need to know everything." We walked to the parking garage and over to a slick gray sedan that screamed: *money*.

I sat in the front. The leather seats and luxurious interior were impressive.

As Garrett drove us out of there, his hand landed on my thigh. It both thrilled and discomfited. I knew lawyers weren't supposed to touch their teenage clients.

I shifted, and his hand moved. Perhaps I'd read too much into it.

He talked as he drove. "The media is in a frenzy, especially since your parents haven't been sighted at all since the morning of the fifteenth."

The last time I'd seen them. If I'd known, I'd have hugged them tighter.

"Have you heard anything at all from them?" he queried.

"How would I? The police took my phone, and I was in a mental ward." With no link to the outside world.

"Is there anywhere they might go? A special place?"

"No." And I didn't like that he'd asked.

"What about family?"

"No family."

"Surely, there's someone we could talk to who might take you in," he cajoled.

"No."

"That's a shame. It'll limit your options."

"I'm almost eighteen. Can't someone stick me in an apartment?"

"Some states will allow it at sixteen, but ours doesn't. Meaning, you'll be placed with someone the government deems suitable until you turn eighteen."

"What if I run away?"

He shrugged. "Is living on the street really better?"

I hated that he might have a point. "What do the cops want from me? I don't know anything."

"They want to make sure that's true. So, they're going to ask you all kinds of questions meant to trip you up."

"Aren't you supposed to stop them from doing that?"

"If you don't know anything, then it's more effi-cient to get this over with." He pulled up to the familiar cop station. "We're here."

As if drawn by a magnet, curiosity-seekers swarmed the car.

Panic filled me. "Can't we go around to the hidden side entrance?"

"Your parents are famous. You'll have to learn to deal with it. We'll start by giving a statement." By *we*, Garrett meant him. He offered a lovely, eloquent speech about an innocent young girl caught up in a terrible situation. I got to stand awkwardly by his side, gazing at my feet, wishing the ground would swallow me, or even better, that I would wake up from this nightmare.

No one interrupted while Garrett spoke, but when he was done, questions fired fast and furiously. While I didn't reply to any of them, I learned a lot by listening.

Apparently, my lawyer had graciously donated his services to the poor young girl caught in a serial killer case web. I was old enough to realize that he was using me for celebrity to advance his career. Whatever. I needed all the help I could get.

Eventually, he held up a hand. "That's all for now. If you'll excuse me, my client needs to give a statement to the police."

Given the choice between rabid reporters and the cops, I practically jogged to the doors of the precinct. My lawyer kept a more sedate pace. They brought us to a different room done up in younger, brighter colors. The chairs were plastic and vivid—a place meant for children.

It felt more awkward than the room with everything bolted down. I recognized the police officer as the one from before. Olsen once again held a binder and appeared impatient as he slapped it down on the short table.

"Browning. I should have known you'd weasel your way into this case."

"Whatever do you mean?" Garrett asked, legs crossed, leaning back, seemingly at ease. "Simply providing a pro bono service to an innocent in what is a horrific case."

"I'd better not hear of anything you see today being leaked."

"Are you accusing me of impeding an investigation?" my lawyer asked, his tone mocking.

"This isn't a joke. These murders are serious."

"One murder. And from what I hear, your case isn't airtight."

It wasn't? How come Garett hadn't mentioned that in the car?

"Think again," muttered Olsen. "Let's start the interview."

We began with the basics. Name. Address. School. Parents. Where did they work? Easy stuff. Then they eased into the tougher bits. Where was I on the following dates? Where were my parents on certain dates?

"Give me my phone, and I'll tell you." I put everything in my electronic agenda.

"Your phone is being held as evidence."

My jaw dropped. "Evidence of what?"

Rather than reply, Olsen went on. "Are your parents Satanists?"

"No."

"Why are there no religious icons in your house?"

"They're atheists."

"Have they ever sacrificed animals?"

My eyes just about fell out of my head. "No."

I exclaimed it often as Olsen asked questions, and my lawyer said nothing.

It took me exploding with, "My parents aren't killers!" for the questioning to stop.

Finally, Garrett stepped in with a drawled, "You're pestering my client."

"We're trying to bring justice to a victim, and she's not helping."

"Is there a victim?" my lawyer queried. "I hear you haven't found a body yet."

"Only a matter of time. We have the video."

The damning footage.

My lawyer shredded that with a casual, "You call that evidence? No one knows where it was shot. You've not actually found a crime scene. Or a body. Meaning, you don't have a case."

"We have the other pentagrams."

"And have you been able to link Abigail's parents to those? Or is that flimsy footage the only evidence you have?"

"We're going to find the basement in that video," Olsen blustered.

"I find it odd that no one has come forth to claim they know where it is yet."

"We're still checking out tips," indicated Olsen.

"Can I see it again?" I asked. I'd had three days to convince myself that it was fake. That it wasn't as damning as they claimed.

In seconds, my lawyer had it running. Garrett paid it no mind. I was to find out later just how viral it had gone.

As it played, I felt numb, removed from the people in it. Yes, those awful, robed people with their hands in the blood wore my parents' faces, but that wasn't them. I didn't recognize my mother and her wide, startled eyes. Or my father with that snarl on his lips.

During the second playback, as the person taking the video slowly descended the steps, I frowned and said, "What is he singing? I can't make out the words."

"Nor can anyone else," Olsen stated. "Most likely some gibberish thing that's supposed to be an ode to Satan."

"Black magic," Garrett added as if it made sense.

"My parents aren't Satanists."

"Are you sure about that?" my own damned lawyer said.

Many fictional stories emerged once the video hit the 'net. The most common theme was that my dad was Satan's priest on Earth, an evil minion who sacrificed nice and decent people to the dark lord. A man who'd turned violent because someone caught him. He looked nothing like the guy who'd tossed me into the air and caught me with a chuckle.

When the video ended, I had to wonder. "Who filmed it?"

"We're still trying to track them down." A disgruntled admission by Olsen.

Which led to me voicing more of my doubts. "What makes you think they weren't indulging in some roleplay?" Never mind the fact that my parents never dressed up. However, I'd rather think they had a fetish for outfits than be stone-cold killers.

Olsen snorted. "I know murder when I see it."

"Do you need to be reminded again that you don't have a body?" Garrett pounced on that.

The cop's expression soured as he had to admit, "Not yet."

"Then it could be some kind of movie. After all, eyes don't glow like the male's did without special effects." My lawyer pointed.

"Trick of the light. That video places them at the crime scene."

"Which you haven't located," Garrett reminded.

"What about the other two pentagrams we found? All the blood?" Olsen insisted.

"Without a body, you can't prove that a crime occurred." My lawyer was smug, but I enjoyed how he argued with the cop.

"If they're so innocent, then why did they disappear? Why haven't they come for their daughter?"

None of the replies to that question made me feel any better.

Why had my parents abandoned me?

Were they actually killers?

Would I follow in their footsteps?

6

CASSIDY SHOWED UP AT THE POLICE STATION, once more apologizing for her lateness. I hadn't realized how long I'd sat in the barren office, waiting. Before leaving, Garett had given me a prepaid phone that I could hook up to Wi-Fi. I spent some time on the internet, catching up on what my lawyer and the cops weren't telling me.

The number of articles, posts, and comments was staggering. I made the mistake of reading some of them before my churning stomach had me searching for cute kitten pics.

Too late. The words I'd read remained seared on my retinas.

Hope they catch those murderers and decapitate them.

Yeah. With a dull knife.

But first rape their ugly ass daughter.

Why did they want to hurt me? I'd done nothing.

I sat in shock and silence on the drive to my temporary home. Cassidy didn't seem to notice.

"I found you a place. Francine is technically retired from the foster care business, but when I told her about the challenge of placing you, she agreed to take you on."

"So I'm a pity case. Great," I grumbled under my breath.

The house was a bungalow, shabby but clean. The inside was old and worn, as well, the carpet rubbed shiny in spots.

Francine turned out to be a woman with a short, silvery haircut and a pear-shaped figure. She took one look at me and said, "Don't give me any trouble, and we'll get along fine."

How had my straight-A ass gone from teacher's pet and honor roll to borderline criminal?

Francine wasn't bad, though. She stayed out of my way, only calling me for food and to make sure I saw my daily list of chores. None took too long, so I spent a lot of time in my room, scouring the web, unable to stop myself from looking at the train crash that was now my life.

Why were people so horrible? I'd done nothing, but the things I read made me hate. Made me wonder if perhaps a kernel of evil existed in me. Because I *did* want to hurt. Scream. Rail at the world and the unfairness of it all.

While I'd been in the hospital, neighbors had come out to say they'd always known there was something wrong with my family. Coworkers said my parents seemed like such nice, normal people. A kid at my school called me the weird nerd girl—way to devalue my hard work and studying.

A supposed witness, who claimed to be the person filming, turned out to be a fake. People loved their tiny moments of fame, which might be why the press kept hounding me. I insisted it was all a mistake. My conviction fell on deaf ears. The longer my parents remained on the lam, the less I believed in their innocence. Surely, they would have stayed to fight if only to be with me.

It didn't help that I kept having dreams of my dad. A man with glowing eyes, telling me that he loved me and how he wished he could take me away but that this was for the best.

Best for whom? Because I certainly wasn't doing very well.

Despite efforts to scrub the video, it went viral. And given that the pentagram crimes stretched over state lines, the FBI came in.

Which led to another round of questioning by

Special Agent Lyle Brunealt, an intense man with a thin combover. He got right to business, his voice firm—not unkind but not friendly either. He didn't care about me. He wanted information.

"Have you heard from your parents?"

"Nope." The honest truth.

"What do you know about the pentagram murders?" he asked.

"Only what they say on the internet. Is it true you've never found any bodies?" According to the documentary, while many pentagrams had been found with blood pools indicating a massacre, nobody had located a single corpse. Testing on the blood confirmed it as human, but the ash in the center of the design? Inconclusive.

"Still no actual victims, I hear. Nor a single DNA match from any of the crime scenes," Garrett offered on a low purr.

Brunealt scowled. "Doesn't mean shit. Transients are hard to track and rarely reported missing."

"Or could it be that no crime was committed?" Garrett said.

"The video says otherwise." Brunealt cleared his throat. "Abigail, did you ever see your parents practice any type of witchcraft?"

"No." Although, they did own a lot of candles,

which I never saw them burn. And yet, every few months, we got a box full.

"Pray to Satan?"

I snorted. "Seriously?"

"Just answer."

"Why? Didn't we already go through this?" How many times would I have to answer the same questions?

"Let's do it again."

On and on it went, the agent asking me dumb shit, me replying to his stupid questions. I knew nothing, but he assumed I lied. He kept waiting for me to trip up. When I didn't, the FBI watched me like a hawk, hoping my parents would come for me or, at the very least, contact me in a way they could trace.

They weren't the only ones who figured Mom and Dad would get in touch. The people who loved me wouldn't have abandoned me—not without some kind of word.

Then again, how could they come near? With so many eyes on me, it would be dangerous for them to approach. And if they'd left me a note at home, I never got it.

The police didn't allow me to return—not even for my stuff—since they considered it a crime scene. Even my bedroom. Although at Garrett's insistence, they allowed my social worker inside to pack me some things, clothes and toiletries, which they then pawed through before letting me have them.

Cassidy had kindly included a picture of my parents and me that I kept on my dresser. The three of us smiling like a happy, normal family. Was my childhood a lie? Because the circumstantial evidence was piling up. The states we'd lived in all had bloody pentagram crime scenes. The other places with similar crime scenes were all close enough to drive.

I already knew my parents had been planning to move again, using my college as an excuse. Would university even be possible now? I'd already had two of my offers rescinded, and I was waiting on the third.

What would happen to me once I graduated and turned eighteen? Where would I go? What would I do? I had no one to turn to because I was alone in the world.

The only saving grace in my life was Garrett, who for some reason, kept me protected. Once everyone realized that I knew nothing, the meetings with law enforcement stopped. I could only say, "I don't know," so many times before they gave up.

The media, though? It took me shaming them to stop the harassment.

Frustrated at how they intruded on my life when

all I wanted to do was wallow in misery, I created my own live video. I cried and claimed that a reporter was blackmailing me. True, actually. He'd said he would paint me as a killer if I didn't send him nude pictures.

The focus shifted as people screamed at the media and railed at how they exploited tragedy and children. They soon moved on to the next scandal. And from that moment on, I remained quiet because I knew how easily the world online could turn into a mob.

Within a few weeks, my celebrity status waned. Cassidy, who'd been fired for selling my story—with embellishments—to a tabloid, was replaced by Mrs. Fitzpatrick, an older lady with gray hair and a formidable bosom. She decided that she didn't like me living with Francine and shifted me to a group home for teens. I was a curiosity for a few days until they realized I wouldn't torture any cats or kill any neighborhood kids.

Yet.

But I swore if the guy with the locker beside mine slapped me again with its door, I might make an exception.

7

AS INTEREST IN MY CASE WANED, SO DID MY visits with my lawyer. Which was fine. He was just a reminder that my life sucked.

Given my group home was across town, I never returned to my school, and I was glad. I'd seen what they were saying online. Mean shit about me. Even my so-called friends—in other words, fucking strangers who never even smiled at me in the halls— gave interviews, claiming they knew my family had issues with no reasoning behind it. The parents were even worse, with one PTA bitch going on and on about the fact that my mom sometimes brought prepackaged goods to the potluck events. That cow didn't mention that those treats tended to disappear before her healthy zucchini, no-gluten, no-sugar, no-fucking-anything-good cake.

I knew I should ignore the online crap, even as I listened to every single interview. Read all the articles. Cried over some of the meanest comments.

I couldn't entirely escape the morbid curiosity that followed me.

Where were the bodies?

Who'd died in those pentagrams?

What were my parents trying to do?

Where were they?

People persisted in thinking I had the answers. The internet sleuths were all convinced that my parents had done it, even though none of the trace evidence collected from the scenes matched anything in our house. As a matter of fact, nothing existed to connect my parents to any of the crime scenes. And they'd yet to find the one in the video, which, depending on which expert you talked to, might have been doctored.

A few people called the tip line, looking to collect the reward by saying they'd found the basement depicted. All those statements turned out to be false.

Just like all the supposed rumors about me were fake.

A killer like her parents.

She chokes out guys when she has sex.

She's pregnant with the Antichrist.

And the more disgusting claimed pregnant with my daddy's baby.

I'd have preferred that people hit me. Bruises would have healed. What they did to my head-space... It broke me for a while.

Suicide, not something I'd ever contemplated before, haunted too many of my waking moments.

Despite changing schools, I couldn't escape the whispers—not in the halls, not in the cafeteria. They talked about me in the group home. Kids younger than me but tougher. I soon discovered a world where fists flew if you dared to object.

I quickly developed thick skin. It didn't stop the barbs—*It's a full moon next week. You gonna sacrifice one of us?*— but it dulled them.

Teeth gritted, heart tucked into a safe room that no one could touch, I went to my new school and did my best to keep my head down and not talk to people. I only had two months left before I graduated. Two months that felt like an eternity, given my parents' reputation followed me.

It amazed me how little it took to be bullied. Merely *existing* in my case. I was shoved into lockers with demands that I show them what my parents taught me.

They taught me to tie my shoes. Ride a bike. Cook very poorly—mostly because I loved watching my dad putter in the kitchen, making me something homemade instead of that store-bought crap. Mom bought the crap because she hated what she called wasting her time on something she could easily afford. But Mom did love her closet. She'd be appalled if she saw my clothes of gray on black, no makeup. I heard people muttering, "Emo freak." I ignored them. I just wished they'd forget I existed.

I made it, week by week, to the goal line of graduation, feeling more and more depressed as it neared. My third-choice college rescinded my admission due to moral concerns.

Assholes. The letters made me burn with rage. Maybe I was a killer like my parents. Because when I read their words, I wanted to light their schools on fire.

My psychiatrist said it was a normal response. Maybe he was a serial killer, too. I sure as hell hoped so because Dr. Werner was so boring. "Tell me, Abby, how are you feeling today?"

If I told him I wanted to peel off his face and stick it to a window like one of those clings you bought during the holidays, would he give me a prescription for pills I could sell? Jobs were scarce. I was working ten hours a week and not saving enough to do anything. I had submitted a last-minute admission to a trade college with no money to pay for it and little time to apply for grants.

"I'm feeling okay." The safest answer with my doctor. I didn't need the group home restricting my food choices again, claiming the salt in my diet made me experience violent thoughts. Ha. What truly made me consider violence was the number of times I'd had to sit in this office or one very similar since my parents went on the lam.

Selfish bastards. It was so unfair. They'd ruined my existence. Took away my happiness and my future.

And they were cruel about it. They'd given me a taste of suburban life, one I'd thought so boring though now wished I could have back. I even missed how my parents rushed me through my breakfast in the morning despite the fact I'd never been late. While doing my homework, I'd have to start over with a fresh sheet at times because of the tears that fell as I recalled Mom showing me how to do my math, then cursing when I told her they didn't do it like that anymore.

"Stupid new math!" she'd rail. "Why couldn't they leave it the way it makes sense?" It drove her nuts. Maybe that was why she'd indulged in sadistic rituals that ended in blood and death.

Perhaps I should mount a challenge against the

new math and hold up a sign that read: *See, it drove my parents to murder*.

Except I still didn't believe they were killers.

The video was the only thing linking them to the pentagram killings, and it had as many people debunking it as believing it. It might have died away, except a week before graduation, someone stumbled across a pentagram in a condemned building. The blood within the shape belonged to the body found slumped beside it. Gerald Huntington. Apparently, he'd worked with my dad.

The cops finally had a body. Now, they just needed to find my parents.

With a body making charges possible, interest in the case resurfaced. Someone scrawled *Slaughter Daughter* on the garage door attached to the group home I lived in. Tina, who owned the place, was actually happy about it because it meant she could charge the state to replace it.

I tried to close my ears to the now very elaborate theories people had had time to construct. The most popular being that Mom and Dad were practicing Satanists, sacrificing people to open a doorway for the dark lord. A cool idea if a supernatural television show, not so neat in real life. People treated me like a fascinating freak instead of a person.

"Did you know?" they'd ask with wide eyes as if they were the first.

I kept my shrugged reply short. "I thought they were atheists with a Christmas tree." Who celebrated epic Halloweens. My dad used to go all out, making us the scariest house on the block and handing out full-sized chocolate bars.

Since the internet already ran wild with the notion that I was the Antichrist, being raised by Satan's loyal servants, I chose to make my reputation even more interesting by starting an online rumor that my parents would return on my eighteenth birthday to sacrifice me and use my virgin blood.

It led to many offers to take my virginity. Boys who'd snicker at me in the halls, sidling close and saying, "Meet me in the locker room after school. I'll save you from your parents."

Idiots. I wasn't a virgin, but I preferred to remain single. Especially since I had no idea how to explain to a potential partner, "By the way, everyone thinks my parents killed people for the devil."

Refusing to let boys take turns saving me meant that even more rumors popped up. I withdrew and took the term *hermit* to new levels. All my case-workers were convinced that something must be wrong with me. Why didn't I have friends? I probably drowned kittens or set dogs on fire. Pulled the wings off flies.

If I did, I could guarantee that no one would ever find the bodies. Couldn't be charged with murder if they never found a corpse.

Why had my parents gotten sloppy? Did they want to get caught?

8

TECHNICALLY, I DIDN'T HAVE TO ATTEND THE last week of school, but I had nowhere else to be. The group home insisted we go, and I did enjoy the French fries in the cafeteria. Although, rumor had it they'd be axed the following year in favor of healthy vegetables.

I enjoyed my fries one by one, dipping the tip of each in ketchup. I kept eating, even as a gaggle of girls flopped on the bench across from me.

"Well, if it isn't Slaughter Daughter, eating her fries dipped in blood." One of them, Bethany, did a bad imitation of a cartoon vampire.

"Such maturity for your age. What are you two?" I said sweetly.

"Ha-ha, funny girl. You going to tell jokes when your parents come to sacrifice you?"

It might have been a better barb if I'd not created the urban legend that spawned it. "Actually, I was thinking of telling them where you live. After all, they're looking for virgins."

Color spotted Bethany's cheeks. "So, you admit it. You do talk to them!"

I rolled my eyes. "If I was in contact, do you think I'd be in this shitty cafeteria, talking to your simple-minded ass?"

"Guess you'll be alone for graduation."

Now that hurt. I'd always imagined the pride on my parents' faces when I graduated. Instead, I'd heard rumors that the cops would be out in full force, hoping Mom and Dad would be stupid enough to come.

They'd better not. Even though I wished they'd give me a sign.

When they finally did, it wasn't a great one. I found it tucked in my locker at the fast food chain place where I worked. The note— in my mother's loopy scrawl on a French fry envelope with a few twenties tucked inside—simply said:

Never forgotten. Always loved.

I didn't feel loved. I felt more alone than ever.

They were alive. They just didn't want me with them.

The time I spent in the group home took forever

and passed in a forgettable blur. I went through the motions, knowing I just had to make it to my eighteenth birthday.

I spent a lot of that time alone, going over every inch of my childhood. Things that had seemed normal, now made me question. I'd always assumed the ax-throwing and jujitsu lessons I took with my dad were because he enjoyed sports and wanted to expose me to several of them.

My mom was a whiz on a computer, and I knew my way around. But now I had to wonder about all those times I'd asked to see the Dark Web, and she'd laughed and said, "Honey, there is no such thing outside the movies."

But all I did was wonder. I didn't do any kind of searches on my parents. Didn't go anywhere that might seem weird. Which meant I rarely left the house. The entire time I spent in custody—also known as the foster care system—I remained aware that my every action was examined with creepy thoroughness.

Everything I did was noted and reported. My exciting life of school, homework, work, and sleep. The third psychologist they made me see didn't make the situation better, claiming I was repressing my natural urges and trying to fool them by pretending to be normal.

I laughed at him and asked if he had fantasies about teenage girls murdering people.

"Do you dream of killing people, Abigail?"

"No."

"Take off your shirt, or I'll tell them you do." The bastard had the nerve to lick his lips.

"Go fuck yourself, creep."

In retaliation, he tried to have me removed from school and placed in an institution for more individualized sessions. I then publicly declared that he was a pedophile trying to get in my pants. I got a new female shrink after that.

I graduated with no one in the crowd to clap when I accepted my diploma, and people unsure if they should cheer me. Next time I went in to work, I found an envelope of cash in my locker. I didn't know how it got there, but I knew who it was from. It didn't completely quell the anger I felt that they hadn't taken me with them, but showed they were paying attention.

It was the last direct contact they made. My mom always said that she wanted me to have a nice, normal life. Joke was on them. It would never be normal again.

9

WHEN I TURNED EIGHTEEN, THE GOVERNMENT couldn't get rid of me fast enough. In their generosity, they dropped me off at a woman's shelter with my knapsack of belongings. I had a few hundred dollars to my name. A name that kept causing trouble. Three days after my arrival, the media found me, and the shelter kindly asked me to leave.

I had enough money to rent a room for the week, but then I was fucked.

The day before I'd be forced to try my luck on the streets, my parents died. And they did so in spectacular, public fashion.

I heard about it on the news when I turned on the television. I held a burger to my lips for the entire length of the clip plus some. Riveting didn't describe it. A drone in the sky followed the speeding blue car, supposedly carrying my parents, as cops chased them. We got a drone's-eye view as the vehicle soared off the cliff. It rolled a few times down the steep, stony embankment before hitting the water.

By the time they dredged it, it held one body that could only be identified by dental records. Mom was dead, and given what'd happened, Dad was ruled gone, as well. I became an orphan for real.

No more pentagrams were found, but interest in me didn't wane overnight. It took a few salacious threads and headlines before it went away.

Life started to suck less. With my parents officially declared dead, I became the sole heir of their estate, although the government tried to keep it from me. Attempted to claim it was ill-gotten gains.

For a fee—because pro bono only happened when a girl was broke—Garrett helped me out again, arguing that having never been charged or convicted, my parents were still deemed innocent by law. They had no official victims or families, just the one dead man with no one to claim him.

I inherited a few hundred thousand, which sounded like a lot until Garrett took a cut, and I did the math. If I was careful, I could live on it and go to school. To be safe, though, I'd get a part-time job for fun money.

The first thing I did once I got the funds squared

away? I applied to have my name changed, then began submitting to colleges that didn't look too hard at my fake high school grades. I applied to places far enough from my hometown that no one would recognize me. It helped that I'd changed my hair color from the red I had been born to black cut into a short bob. I wore bulky sweaters, jeans, and thick-rimmed glasses. I spent two years studying hard and keeping my nose clean. No drugs in my veins. No booze in my liver. While I dated a bit, I never got too serious with anyone.

I wanted to be in control at all times. By the end of year two, I began to relax, which was when a nosy reporter tracked me down. The asshole revived the whole Slaughter Daughter mess and turned me into a campus freak overnight. I might have toughed it out, except winters in Maine were rough. Given I had the means and no attachment to any place, I decided to transfer south. Managed a year before I got exposed again.

But I wasn't giving up, dammit. I'd been good with my money, and I wanted my degree.

I chose a school on the East Coast, nestled in a midsized town in Maine, and agreed to redo some of my courses as part of a two-year program thanks to the curriculum differences.

The school sat closer than I liked to my original

hometown, but as I had recently realized, I couldn't hide from my past. Although, as I looked out over the sprawling campus of green acres cut by friendly walking paths, I wondered if it was time to stop running. If I were going to deal with this shit my entire life, perhaps I should stand my ground.

If only confrontation didn't make me quiver.

Long strides took me across the university grounds. I'd memorized a map ahead of time, so I knew where to go for my dorm: the Hennessy House. My knapsack with all my worldly goods hung on my shoulder, my last place having been vandalized before I could move out. I planned to buy some stuff once I had somewhere to put it.

The sign on the left indicated *Hen s y use*. Missing a few letters. The campus wasn't one of the newer ones, and the dorm I'd managed to find was from an older era. It stood blocky and utilitarian with its crumbling red brick façade, three stories with a pitched and gabled roof. Home sweet home for the next year. More if they didn't kick me out.

Having been asked to leave a few residences once my name became known, I should have been used to new starts. I still needed to take a deep breath before entering the dorm. Tension filled my frame. New places, new faces, it never got any easier.

A small crowd milled in the common area, their

voices loud, everyone looking to outdo, to be the *cool one* in the dorm. To that end, it was a competition to be the most relaxed—from the most disreputable and baggy track pants to the faded sweatshirts and T-shirts. Lots of rubber shoes and flip-flops, but also the most ridiculous slippers—unicorns, giant bear feet, and more. Hair unbrushed or held in intentionally sloppy buns.

I hated dorms. Too crowded and pretentious for me. But at the same time, I didn't need a fancy pad, just a bed to call mine until I could graduate and get a job that would pay for my living expenses. I wanted to leave the money in the bank as backup.

Easy-fucking-peasy. Funny how when I was younger, the use of curse words seemed so... well...*bad*. And this even though my parents cursed. My mom had an especially profane potty mouth, but she was also one of the smartest women I knew. It made sense when, later on, I read an article that said that smart people cussed. I liked to think I was better than your average Joe Schmoe.

Fuck me, I was stalling instead of finding my room. I managed to inch sideways, hugging the wall, not meeting anyone's gaze. Shyness was only part of it. New places freaked me out. It took me time before I got comfortable, and it wouldn't happen getting friendly with the wall.

Shoulders back, I aimed for the person holding a clipboard. About my age, she had her hair pulled back in a ponytail with tortoise-rimmed glasses perched on her nose. Her T-shirt displayed some kind of cute animal with a saying meant to be edgy. It clashed with her fruit bowl leggings and neon flip-flops. I could only aspire to care so little about matching in public. I kept few clothes, and they were all tame in coloring so they could be interchangeable. Practical, right?

Boring also came to mind.

"Name?" the girl asked, only briefly meeting my gaze. No smile. She'd probably worn it out a dozen students ago. It amazed me sometimes how vocal and discontent people could get over the slightest things.

"Abby. Abby Baker." My new, simplified name.

I'd opted to change my name only slightly, just enough that my legal papers were easy to shift. I reverted to my mother's maiden name, which was ordinary enough to slide by without people automatically making a connection.

"Abby Baker." She ran her finger down the list. "Three-C."

"Who's my roommate?"

She met my gaze briefly. "That's private information."

EVE LANGLAIS

"But we're sharing a space. I'm going to find out soon enough."

"If your roommate chooses to divulge. Just like it's your choice whether or not you impart any kind of personal information."

"That's cold," I replied.

She stiffened. "Your aggressiveness is making me uncomfortable."

I moved before I was the one triggered and did something to that ponytail of hers. Might be time to see the doctor again for some happy pills. I didn't like relying on drugs, but shit was getting a little tense of late. My temper a little more volatile.

While I'd yet to actually snap and hurt anyone, I came close at times. Which then made me wonder... is murder hereditary like old Doctor Johnson used to think?

Room Three-C was obviously on the third floor. No elevator meant the many steps would give me a daily workout, thus giving me more time to study instead of exercising. I called this positive thinking because, really, I wanted to curse and kick up a fuss.

The first-floor landing door was propped open to reveal a hallway packed with people who seemed like kids to me. You know, because I was so old. I probably sat somewhere in the middle, and yet I felt a gazillion times older as I watched their young, animated faces. The din of their loud talking hit me in a muddled mess. As if that weren't already noise enough, music played from one of the eight single-occupancy rooms, people bopping to it.

A lively bunch. A little too lively for me.

The second floor had a more serious air with someone playing classical music on a violin. Then there was the third floor, which felt a bit smaller given they'd built it in the attic, and it had a sloping roof—probably to ensure the snow could slide off. While there appeared to be less space, it was blissfully quiet.

The converted attic space only had two doors, which meant fewer of us sharing a bathroom. Personally, I could have gone with having my own, but I was too late when I applied to get a single with facilities. Maybe I should stop being so stingy and find something nearby in town. But that would involve living on my own. While I might not interact much with the dorm kids, when I huddled in my bed at night, and the anxiety came creeping in, it helped to know that someone was across the room or down the hall.

I entered my room and immediately noticed that the slanted ceiling was lowest by the headboards. Mental note: No bouncing on the mattress. I'd whack myself for sure. A window sat between the beds, partially covered by a battered desk with a single plastic chair, repaired with duct tape.

Fancy. The desk had scorch marks from a previous smoker. Crud of dirt or mold filled the cracks in the windowsill. The light flickered when I crossed the room, and I eyed it suspiciously.

I'd been in my share of crappy places. This was worse than usual.

Guess I should count myself lucky that even though there was no closet, my yet-to-be-seen roomie and I each had a tall dresser, unmatched and probably salvaged from a curb on garbage day. One had chipped purple paint. Mine was scratched walnut wood stain. The *piece de resistance* that made this whole room bearable? Sitting at the foot of the bed was a bench that opened. Be still my heart. Good thing I didn't own more than two pairs of shoes.

Not exactly spacious quarters. Especially for sharing.

Maybe if I put glow-in-the-dark star-shaped stickers on the ceiling, it wouldn't be so bad.

Don't be a cheap cunt. Something I'd heard in a movie recently. For some reason, the phrase had stuck with me. Hoarding all the dough wouldn't do me any good if I died of absolute misery.

I deserved better. Hadn't my last shrink told me I should stop punishing myself? I didn't see saving dollars rather than spending it on stuff as smart, but apparently, it could also be construed as monetary flagellation.

What could it hurt to spend a little of my inheritance? First thing after I settled into my classes, I'd see about relocating. My inheritance was enough, especially if I got a job, to allow a little splurging on myself and still have some left over for the future.

I deserve better. I repeated it to myself, trying my best to believe it. Then I remembered the note stuffed under my last dorm room door. The message on it was an angry red scrawl, the slash of the marker violent in its vehemence.

Murderous cunt. You should be the one rotting in the ground.

Words hurt—even false ones.

I set my knapsack down on the bench. All my worldly possessions in one overstuffed bag. After my room got ransacked, I'd ditched most of my things when I moved. Clothes were easy to replace, and toiletries could be gotten at just about any store. The things I truly needed were my bank card, laptop, and phone—which I should note was not to talk to anyone but because I could hotspot my computer with it. I didn't trust open networks. I went to the window and crouched to peek outside.

The door to the room crashed open.

I almost gave myself a concussion on the low ceiling. I whirled and moved to a safer spot to see a woman walk in, shaking her head.

"You have got to be kidding me. No. This won't do. Not at all." She was very pretty with her dark hair shining and smoothed past her shoulders, tan skin, and full lips. She wore a blouse embroidered with thread as vivid as the gloss on her mouth. A purse hung from her forearm, and judging by its fancy stitching, I'd wager it had some kind of flashy brand name. My knapsack came from Walmart. It sported a unicorn because fantasy creatures drew attention, and thieves preferred to avoid that.

The newcomer planted her hands on her hips and went on a rant in a melodic language, still not having addressed me directly. I wasn't sure if that was a good or a bad thing. For all I knew, she was ranting about my presence.

Despite wondering if I'd be safer diving out the window, I ventured a cautious, "Hi."

Her gaze narrowed in on me. "Who are you?"

"The roommate?" I said it almost fearfully. If she didn't like the room, what would she think of me? My well-worn jeans had a hole in the knee and a belt loop hanging. My T-shirt, picked up at some museum, had faded from being washed. My boots were comfortable and worn-in enough that I could

just slip my feet into them. I kept my brown hair—
the natural red of it died to hide—pulled back.
Nothing fancy. My face was clean. No makeup.

Definite appraisal filled her eyes as she perused
me up and down. "I am Kalinda, your roommate." A
pretty name. I went to introduce myself, only she
kept talking, turning to take in the entirety of the
room and exclaiming, "A tiny space like this, and
they think to split it in two?"

"I don't need much."

"There's 'not much,' and then there's this."
Kalinda snorted. "This is not a room for ladies.
Utterly unacceptable. We will require something
else." She turned on her heel and took a few steps
before snapping, "Don't sit there meekly accepting
the insult, come with me. We're upgrading accom-
modations."

We?

10

THE VERY IDEA OF BEING A *WE* WITH ANYONE seemed strange. I also knew better than to let myself get swept along. "I'm fine staying here."

"No, you're not. Don't be stubborn. Let's go." Kalinda exited.

I turtle-walked to the door, convinced that she'd disappeared in a whirlwind of determination. I bit my lip before I peeked out. My gaze widened as I saw her standing just outside, tapping her foot. "I don't like waiting."

"Sorry?" I ventured. "I told you I don't need a new room."

"Of course, we do. We can't share that tiny space."

There was that *we* again. We couldn't be a we. Not with my past. The moment she found out I was the infamous Slaughter Daughter in all those memes, she'd ditch me quicker than a vape in the bathroom at school when a teacher walked in.

Personally, I didn't see the allure in smoking nicotine in stupid flavors, but I did enjoy some CBD oil from time to time when I needed to sleep. I'd have to find myself a shop that sold it. Insomnia was a bitch.

"Are you a fourth year, too?" I asked because it was hard to peg her age.

"Nope. First year." A reply that explained her shock at the room. She'd soon discover that dorms weren't the nicest of places unless you attended an expensive, swanky school.

She tapped on her phone as we trotted down to the first floor, and she managed not to break her ankle, even in heeled boots. Despite my lack of wardrobe sense, I recognized someone dressed to the nines in tight jeans, strategically ripped—unlike mine, which involved hitting the pavement and tearing out a knee—and well-tooled, leather boots. She could have stepped off a magazine cover; she was picture-perfect—unlike my messy ass—and remained under the impression that we were moving out together.

Maybe she thought grunge was trending again.

I felt the need to argue. "I don't think the college

will have anything better. Which is fine. I'm okay. And it does seem quiet up there, which is a plus." I made a face as we passed the zoo on the first floor.

"Quiet should be for study times only. Weekends should get noisy. It's a known rule that you are required to have some fun while at college."

"I'm more interested in graduating. I'm not a big partier."

"Because you haven't met the right people." She cast me a quick glance and a smile.

I should put a stop to it. She wouldn't even be contemplating helping me if she knew who I truly was. Yet at the same time, I was supposed to be about starting over. I wasn't Abigail Smith, infamous Slaughter Daughter. I was Abby Baker, owner of a high school diploma, a small heiress with a trust fund of almost half a million dollars—part of which I'd invested in guaranteed return stocks. I did wonder where the money came from. We'd not lived richly. On the contrary, my parents had boring office jobs, and we lived in a suburban house.

Was that part of their cover? Appear mundane and ordinary because they had a double life?

Hard to believe my dad, who kicked the lawn-mower and claimed it hated him, might be a dangerous criminal. Or my mom, who kept wearing her winter boots with the hole because they were still good. Thinking of my parents reminded me that I should be honest now before this woman took things any further.

"Listen, you should know I've got a past. Hooking up with me isn't the best idea."

Kalinda's dark-lashed gaze met mine as she snorted. "I shall choose who I spend time with. Do you believe in animal testing for makeup?"

"No."

"Then there is nothing so awful I can't handle it," was her breezy reply. "I assume you're okay with at least one set of stairs. What about closet space? I'm not sure they have any rooms with a walk-in."

I didn't have enough clothes for a walk-in. "You seriously want us to get a place? Together?"

"You're interesting." She tilted her head.

"You barely know me." I felt a need to ruin my mystique.

"Which makes it even more fun." Her phone pinged, and she bent to reply.

After three years of doing shit on my own, it was kind of fascinating to see someone who took charge and knew how to get things done. And, even better, was using it to help me out.

She tucked her phone away and said, "We'll send someone for your luggage."

I adjusted my knapsack. "This is all I have."

She literally shuddered. "Oh no, you don't. We will have to fix that."

I almost laughed at her utter horror. "Listen, if you're serious about getting a place off-campus, could it be within walking distance?" Which might not be cheap, but if we split the cost, then doable.

"Walking?" Her nose wrinkled. "I've got a car we can share. And I will insist on a maid. I do not scrub toilets."

My lips twitched. "Don't tell me we'll need a chef, too."

She glanced at me, cool and sophisticated, seeming decades older than me. "I'll be doing most of the cooking. Can't have anyone trying to poison us."

"My dad used to say the same thing about packaged food," I said without feeling the sharp pang I used to.

"Your dad is a wise man."

I was proud of myself. I didn't burst out laughing.

As we exited the dorm, I looked behind me at the clipboard person. "Shouldn't we tell them we're leaving so they can reassign the room?"

"No. We're keeping it. We should have something on campus that we can use in case of emergency."

"You mean like a mid-afternoon power nap between classes."

"Naps. Rendezvouses. A stash for stuff." She smiled. "You never know when you'll need to hide and heal from the cruel world." Not the kind of thing you'd expect to hear from someone gorgeous and confident.

She walked to the curb and the prettiest, shiniest Jeep I'd ever seen. It was teal with black trim. The top was down, and in the first five minutes after we took off, I fought to grab my hair and keep it from being whipped from my head. The woman drove fast enough to leave a smooth shave.

"Where are we going?" I yelled as she zoomed down a campus road at probably three times the speed limit.

"Taking us to our new place."

"Already?" That was kind of quick.

"I contacted some friends in town, and it just so happens they have two open rooms we can have."

"Who are these friends?" It occurred to me only now that I was a fucking moron getting in a car with a virtual stranger. What if I'd walked into a trap? It had happened before—invited by a girl in my class to study. Instead, I found myself surrounded by people who thought it funny to ring a bell in my face and scream, "Confess!" I'd watched that show and counted myself lucky that I'd walked out with all my clothes.

"Listen, I appreciate the trouble, but I don't think—"

Kalinda slammed to a stop. "We're here."

I didn't concuss myself, but I almost lost my tongue as I bit it. I gaped at the lovely, old, two-story house she'd parked in front of. I wondered which level we'd be looking at. Emerging from the Jeep, she sauntered up the steps without hesitation.

"This is the place?" I looked around and noted the fine location. The college was maybe a twenty-minute walk, which was eminently doable. If it rained, I could overpay for an Uber or borrow the Jeep. I aimed it a loving, covetous look.

"Yes. I've been here before to visit my friends and can assure you it is much nicer than that cesspool they call a dorm." She visibly shuddered.

"Are you sure they have room for both of us?"

"Oh, Abby, don't be so silly. I wouldn't have brought you here if they didn't."

It was only then that I realized she knew my name. Had I told her? I could have sworn I hadn't. "How do you know my name?"

"They told me when I was getting checked in for that cell they call a room."

That brought a frown. "Told you? That..." —

Don't say bitch, don't say bitch — "bitch told me privacy rules meant she couldn't divulge yours."

A wide smile pulled at Kalinda's full lips. "When I ask for something, I get it. Never take no for an answer."

No kidding.

She sauntered through the front door without knocking.

As for me, I hesitated. Could it be a trap? It was certainly possible, at least according to fear, my constant companion. I glanced down the street. Only twenty minutes back to the dorm.

Kalinda stuck her head back out. "Are you coming or not?"

Curiosity moved my feet, even as my heart proved to be a leaden, heavy thing in my chest. *Please, don't let this be a trick.* The relief almost sighed out of me when I walked in and noticed that just the pair of us stood in the large, two-story hall.

The inside of the house, like the outside, exuded an old grandeur, the kind that involved waist-high wainscoting painted white and gleaming wood floors the same shade and shine as the trim, balustrade, and steps. The foyer was large enough to have a floating table in the center with a vase of flowers—real ones, not plastic. The space spanned two stories, and overhead, the staircase railing split and circled around.

Fancy.

"Is this a sorority?" I asked. I'd not seen a sign.

My determined friend sniffed. "No. The college banned those kinds of clubs. It's just a house, rented to college students and staff."

"Which means, you gotta share the space." The deep voice had me turning to see a guy leaning against the jamb of a wide, arched doorway. He was tall and lanky with dark hair tumbling over his forehead. His jaw held a slight stubble. He wore a button-down shirt and khakis, yet still managed a somewhat rugged, disreputable appearance. It might have had something to do with the hint of a smirk on his lips.

My companion cast him a glance. "We both know you're not the type to share."

"Let's be fair, neither are you." He winked at her, then eyed me. Thoroughly. The guy had sinfully thick and dark lashes. "Hey. Name's Jag. Who are you?"

"Abby. Who else, you idiot? We were just texting about her." My new friend rolled her eyes.

"Does Abby not speak for herself?"

Rather than reply, Kalinda asked, "Is her room ready?"

Jag's jaw tensed. I almost laughed.

Especially since Kalinda added a snarky, "Well?"

"Both rooms have been checked for stains and possible leftover dirty rags from the previous occupants." Jag offered an evil grin.

"Increased your pornographic collection?" Kalinda arched a brow.

"No need for pictures and videos when I can get the real thing anytime, anywhere."

The conceit in this one was strong. I couldn't help a snicker.

"And she almost deigns to speak." He clapped.

"Why do you care if I talk or not?" The sass emerged unchecked.

"Always good to make sure language won't be a barrier."

"Don't expect to hear me much."

"Why ever not?"

I shrugged. "Not much to say."

"Only because she thinks she's shy," Kalinda interjected. "I'm going to fix that."

"I'm not broken," I muttered, which wasn't entirely true.

"Aren't you lucky Kalinda has decided to make you her next project?" Jag drawled.

"You are so annoying," Kalinda declared, moving to the steps. "And the reason I was avoiding living here."

He snorted. "As if you could have lived in a dorm, princess."

She cast him a glare hot enough to scorch. "Come, Abby. You can check out your room while Jag checks to see how far it is from the bridge to the water when he jumps."

"Ouch. You wound me," he said, clutching his chest.

He looked more amused than insulted as I followed Kalinda up the steps. The second floor was just as old-school lavish as the first. There were five doors and a circular set of stairs tucked into a narrow hall, going higher. Another attic room.

I started for the steps, only to have Kalinda say, "Where are you going? Your room is here." She pointed to the door in the middle on our left. "That one is yours. I've got the one next to it." She pointed past the one she'd indicated as mine.

"Are all the rooms occupied?"

She nodded. "You met Jag. He's in the attic. Then we've got Mary, Peter, Cashien, and Jackson."

A co-ed house, in other words. I was fine with that. Especially as the doors all bore keypads. "How do I get in?"

"Code 666. You can reset it to something else later."

I bit my lip. An understandably high-school response to the number of the beast.

With a quick press of my finger, I set it to beep. Three times and...click, the door unlocked. I gaped as I walked into a room that boasted great space.

"It's not a master suite, but I guess it will do." I hadn't realized Kalinda had come up beside me.

I finally had to admit the truth. "I might not be able to afford this." The dorm was costing me six hundred a month plus food. This would be over a thousand, easy.

So, I understandably blinked when she said, "Seven fifty. Plus, there are groceries delivered every week. There is a house app to add items to the list."

An app? Strangely efficient. I stepped into the palatial space. "I might never leave."

"Don't be silly. This is college. You'll have to leave if you want to adventure."

Adventure? Not me. I just wanted to finish college and have a nice, normal life.

It lasted a week.

11

THAT FIRST DAY, ALL SEEMED GOOD. IT DIDN'T take me long to unpack. I was done within twenty minutes, spent another ten admiring my bathroom. All mine. No sharing.

Knock.

"Come in."

The door clicked, and Kalinda entered. "You didn't change your code."

"I will."

"Just came to say dinner will be at seven."

"You don't have to feed me. I can fend for myself." As she stared at me, I bit my lip and said, "Unless you like to cook and have too much, then I'm happy to eat it."

She nodded. "Good. Seven, then."

She left, and I plotted a map of all my classes, which I used to do a practice walk around campus to familiarize myself. Knowing where things were tended to center me, to help with the panic.

I spent that day orienting myself before I explored the house. Kalinda had the room beside mine. On the other side of me was a petite woman, Mary, an exchange student from China with slightly accented English and short, spiked hair tinted a vivid pink. I ran into her when I checked out the kitchen.

She grinned. "Nice to meet you. I'm Mary. If you need anything hacked, let me know." She seemed friendly, but the word *hacked* scared me. My cover wasn't good enough to withstand scrutiny.

At dinner that night, I met Cashien, an assistant professor in the law program. And Peter, a history major. Jag and Kalinda were enrolled in science programs. Me? I studied dead people. Forensic science. Fascinating field. Jackson was absent.

The main floor of the dorm house consisted of a massive living room that could be closed in the middle to create two spaces. There was also a dining room that could seat a dozen, and a giant kitchen with the continent of all islands. We even had a yard of sorts, if you considered an enclosed space of smooth concrete and not a speck of green to be seen a yard. Cashien puffed on his vape out there, curls of smoke emerging from his full lips.

The place was furnished—as in bed, sheets, towels, dishes. Yet over the next two days, extras appeared in my room: fluffy pillows, a mini-fridge filled with my favorite drinks, and a microwave with a giant box of popcorn beside it. I'd found paradise.

Before classes started hardcore, I learned about the campus and all the services, found a place that made a souvlaki that reminded me of our Friday night family tradition before my parents turned out to be suspected murderers on the lam, and a gym where I could beat on a bag and not be called a killer. I almost relaxed, and even managed to sleep almost eight hours each night.

Classes began, and things were fine at first. I sat in the fourth row for each class and listened to my professors, took tons of notes on my laptop. In between lessons, I worked on my homework and tried to get ahead. Found a part-time job in a cupcake shop.

I kept myself busy. When I wasn't working, I studied. True to her word, Kalinda—don't shorten it to Kali or Dina, although she would accept being addressed as *princess*—kept us well-fed. Each evening at seven o'clock, a bell chimed, and whoever was home went and ate in the dining room. Half the time, I had no idea what she made. It was delicious. I took to grabbing leftovers to bring to college the next day, especially since I skipped breakfast.

I rarely saw my other roommates—especially the elusive Jackson—other than meals, which suited me fine. They said hi. I said hi. Strangers in the night. It was perfect. Even at dinner, they tended to eat, be on their phones, or jab verbally at each other. Kalinda talked at me, and I replied in between inhaling food. Then I ran off to study.

I should have been happy. Instead, as the days passed, my tension coiled. I took to taking long walks, but they weren't enough to deal with my anxiety or my conviction I'd be recognized. I kept waiting for the inevitable, for someone to point and say, "It's Slaughter Daughter."

Who knew? Maybe I'd be asked to sign an autograph again. At least the number of freaks trying to screw me dropped once I got rid of all my digital access—no more dick pics for me! I didn't get why they thought sending me an image of their junk was sexy.

A cheesecake drizzled in caramel? That made me lick my lips. A guy's purple warrior that he drew a happy face on? I could see why Lizzie got out an ax. Should have heard what my last shrink had to say about that.

My anxiety wasn't helped by the belief that I was being watched. Paranoia, obviously, since I never caught anyone actively starting at me. Yet, more often than not, my skin prickled when I was out and about.

After a quiet weekend dodging Kalinda's insistence that I go out, I readied for week two of classes.

Monday morning, during my first class, it happened.

"I'm telling you, it's her." I heard the loud whisper and did my best not to react. They could be talking about anyone. I knew the breathing exercise to do when paranoia loomed.

"Fuck you," the guy's companion replied. "No way that's her. Too young. She'd be like a bajillion now. Didn't that happen like twenty years ago?"

"The pentagram thing has been going on forever, dude. But her parents got snared a few years ago."

I slouched in my seat as I realized they were indeed talking about me.

Of course, this would be the morning my professor arrived late. The whispers rose loud enough for me to realize that people buzzed about something, and too many for me to truly make out anything they said. But I could imagine.

Just like I knew what they were doing, tapping furiously on their phones and tablets. Internet searches meant the hum of whispers turned into outright laughter, shock, and exclamations. It was the not-so-subtle, "I don't feel safe, we need to report her," that caused me to snap.

I couldn't endure another year of this. I didn't even want to deal with it for one minute. I stood as the professor, Mr. Santino, walked in.

Since class started on a Tuesday, this was the first time I'd seen him. By most measures a young guy, maybe in his early to mid-thirties. But old compared to me.

His striking blue eyes met mine as I shuffled from my seat. Intense. They oddly reminded me of my dad.

The glance shifted from me to the humming crowd. Could he hear them? Did he know they talked about me?

The shame of it heated my cheeks. Would I ever be free?

I made it to the aisle when the professor spoke, his voice cutting through the din. "Anyone who thinks that a class on the Repercussions of Judgment by Social Media Pundits is the right place to discuss a student in this class, needs to depart. If you cannot show any kind of ethics, then you don't belong here."

Most conversations died down, except for a murmur behind me. I didn't turn around, but my professor stared until there was dead-silence.

"The three of you in the back, wearing those winter hats when it's not even fall, are excused."

"What? You can't do that. I paid for this class." The speaker sounded quite shocked.

"You also signed a contract for conduct, which means I can and *have* expelled you from my course. Out."

The boys grabbed their things with grumbles—and I imagined glares—before exiting.

The professor took a moment to eye everyone left. "This course is about discussing the adverse effect that social media can have on reputations. Of the way rumor and innuendo and doctored memes have destroyed lives without any actual fact. The point of this course is to show the dangers of it. Which means, anyone caught engaging in the spread of such false and inflammatory statements will find I have no tolerance for it. Have I made myself clear?"

You could have heard an earbud fall, it got so quiet.

The blue gaze met mine again. Dared me to leave. Mr. Santino had just addressed my problem without once saying my name. Despite my racing heart, some of my panic abated. It made me happy I'd chosen this class, which I didn't technically need. But if anyone knew what it was like to be roasted on the internet...

I sat back down and listened to him talk. His introduction was no-nonsense.

"I am Professor Joseph Santino. You may call me 'professor.' I am not Joe, nor am I your friend. I won't meet anyone for drinks, nor will I see you alone in my office. If you need to speak to me about class, I am here for ten minutes after. Anything else can be discussed via email."

I listened raptly as he showed, without names or identifying images, an example of a life destroyed by the internet. He pointed out the way it spread beyond the truth and how it affected the victim of the bullying. I recognized the story and wondered if I should worry about my past being a case sample at some point.

That fear was partly why I remained behind when the hour ended, and the students streamed out. I gathered my knapsack, now much lighter, given it only carried snacks, a sweater, and my computer. I remained seated, ignoring curious stares, until everyone was gone except for the professor.

Mr. Santino packed away his materials before

leaning against his podium with arms crossed. "You wanted to speak with me, I assume."

"Yes." Then I was tongue-tied. How to say, "Thank you," and at the same time, beg he not use my story?

"Well?" he queried. Brisk, terse, as if I made him uncomfortable. That made two of us.

"Thank you for standing up for me."

"I didn't do it for you." He sounded unusually harsh, and I almost fled.

I mustered up the nerve to say it in a rush, "I don't want you using me as an example in class."

Santino's brow arched. "What makes you think I would? Did I not admonish the class to not treat you as a curiosity?"

"Yes, but..." I trailed off.

"But your story is a classic example, correct? Poor teenage girl, vilified for the actions of her parents to the point it is following her years later."

I nodded.

"Firstly, it wouldn't be ethical to use it as an example, given you're enrolled not only in my class but also this college. Second, you are an example of someone thriving past the bullying."

"How do you figure that?" I blurted.

"You have managed to attend college with

decent grades." He ticked his fingers. "While not wealthy, you have inherited enough to keep you comfortable."

"How do you know all this?"

"Just because I won't use you as an example doesn't mean I'm not aware of your existence."

My lips pressed into a line. "I really wish they'd leave me alone."

"Your infamy will never fully disappear. Decades from now, someone will still recall your parents' case."

"That's not exactly encouraging." I couldn't help but sound pathetically plaintive.

"It's today's reality. Scandals live forever."

"Unless we get hit with a really big EMP pulse." I blamed the internet for the majority of my problems.

He crossed his arms as he leaned back. "Some would enjoy the notoriety and try to cash in on it."

"Cash in how? People think my parents are serial killers. A bunch of them think I helped them handle the bodies."

"Did you?"

"No," I sputtered.

"Then you know it's lies. Lies only affect us if we allow them to."

"Have you ever been bullied?" I asked. Never mind the fact that he taught a class on it.

"If you're going to launch into a tearful tirade about how hard it is, stop." He held up a hand. "Being attacked, even if only socially and verbally, is devastating. No doubt about it. However, how you react is a choice. If you're miserable, then you're choosing to be miserable."

Funny how in that moment he reminded me of my dad. Except my dad was dead, and the professor was just some random dude pissing me off.

"Actually, I'm angry most of the time. But when I tell people to fuck off, that usually makes things worse." Because then they freaked out and claimed Slaughter Daughter was going to get them. At times, I wished I could.

His lips twitched. "Don't let the reactions of small-minded people deter you."

"Those small-minded people are everywhere," I grumbled.

"You're whining, Ms. Smith."

"Actually, it's Baker now."

"Your mother's maiden name."

"You really did study me. Planning next year's curriculum?"

He shook his head. "No, but I won't deny your parents' situation is fascinating to someone like me.

Here is a case where they were completely convicted in the court of opinion and, by extension, you were, as well. Which is odd. Children are usually seen as victims lucky to survive."

"It's because, when I don't dye my hair, it's red," I pointed out. "It's an inborn instinct to assume that redheads are capable of wicked things."

"We're all capable of great wickedness. Let me ask you, as I see you're now a brunette, has that changed people's perceptions of you when the truth of your parentage emerges?"

"No."

"Then what is the point of a disguise if it doesn't work?"

"Maybe I like the color." I tossed my head.

"More like you think you can hide who you are. Which is why each time you're discovered, it's more calamitous than it needs to be."

"Being me leads to being asked to leave dorms, classrooms, even coffee shops."

"And? If you don't like it, then use your notoriety to draw attention to the injustice of it."

"I don't want to draw attention."

"What you want and reality are two different things, Ms. Baker."

"I want people to stop making assumptions about me."

"Then don't hide. Let them see you and have their foolishness revealed."

"Easy for you to say." I couldn't help but sound bitter.

For a moment, he paused as if he'd say something else, then his expression hardened. "Sorry, Ms. Baker. If you'll excuse me, I have an appointment. I'll see you in class next week."

He probably would, seeing as how he was super interesting. More than that, he understood my situation. "Could we talk more about my case outside of class?" I asked, wanting to extend the bond we appeared to be developing.

Only to be firmly put in my place. "Ms. Baker, I thought I made myself clear on my stance on any fraternization outside of class time."

With that, he took his case and left.

While Santino wasn't the only professor with a policy of inaccessibility, the rejection stunned. Enough that I brought it up with Kalinda when I helped her with dinner by washing vegetables.

"Whatever happened to teachers mentoring students in need?" I complained.

"Can you blame them?" Kalinda retorted. "They don't have a choice but to cover all the angles when it comes to impropriety or the appearance of. Accusations can tank their careers."

"Isn't it kind of overboard, though?"

"Not really. And it's kind of fascinating to watch. The more overcautious they become, the more scrutiny is heightened. The standards raised higher."

"Considering it's usually women being exploited by older men, it's probably not a bad thing."

Kalinda snorted. "Look at you, giving our sex a pass. We are just as capable of seducing to get what we want."

"But less likely," I muttered as I scrubbed the carrots, not trying to get into a pissing match argument over culpability, but apparently unable to stop myself.

"Do you have any idea how many women are attracted to men in power? Especially teachers. It's almost like an aphrodisiac. When those women go after their profs, is it still the man's fault?" she asked.

"Yes," I said, "because they know they have to say no. It's part of their contract, and has to do with ethics."

"Ethics." The snorted words came from Peter as he entered the kitchen. "A fancy word used by some to justify their words and actions when and if someone does something they personally disapprove of."

"Ethics are usually created by a group of people," I remarked.

"Groups always have a leader putting out their version of what they think is right," Peter argued. He might be a history major, but he enjoyed debating, and looked more lawyer-ish than Cashien in his crisp suit and close-cropped hair. He never had a five-o'clock shadow. Unlike Cashien and his more flamboyant style. Jag looked ready to start a bar fight at any time, whereas Jackson, the other guy in the group, always wore dark tracksuits.

"You're implying that ethics is a cult mentality," I argued, just because it was fun to get Peter going.

"That is actually an apt description. For example, if one looks at religion, how things are interpreted depends on who is preaching."

"And a good preacher will convince his congregation that everyone is a sinner, and they can atone by putting more money in the pot." I had a rather acerbic opinion about them, mostly because my parents had always scoffed at churches, calling them leeches and problem-makers.

"Which comes back to the point that ethics is subjective. Contracts can demand a teacher not get involved with a student. However, should that student prove aggressive in intent, then can a professor truly be held responsible when placed under undue sexual duress?" Peter snared a carrot, received a slap from Kalinda, and fled out the back door.

I blinked after him. "Did he just make a case for a teacher being innocent of sexual impropriety?"

"With his grasp of history, he'd have made a great defense lawyer," she stated.

Especially since he saw guilt as subjective.

12

THAT NIGHT, I DREAMED OF MY DAD. IT HAD been a while, and yet he looked as I remembered. Which made me angry.

Get out of my head, I yelled at him.

He said nothing. Just stared at me with a sad expression.

I woke feeling bad and then cursed myself for it. Why had he reappeared to haunt me now? Why couldn't I let go?

I made it through week two, knowing my notoriety had spread by the number of people eying me and the sudden increase in party invitations—which I ignored as I lacked any interest in being a fetish object for them to gawk at or try to fuck.

Saturday rolled around, and after I'd helped

clean up after dinner, Kalinda announced, "I'm going out."

"Okay." Smart thing for her to ensure that someone knew. "Where're you going? Will you be back tonight? What's an emergency number if something happens?" I asked, ticking off the things I should know.

"What's with all the questions?" She pulled off her apron.

"Isn't that why you're telling me? So if something happens, the cops know where to start looking?"

She blinked at me with beautiful, thick lashes. "Don't you dare call the cops if I don't come home one night."

"What if it's been twenty-four hours?"

"No. You tell Cashien or Mary. Anyone in this house. Not law enforcement."

"Okay," I agreed, not even sure why I'd insisted. I hated the cops. Didn't trust them one bit. "Have fun."

"What are you doing tonight?" she asked.

"Studying." What else was there for me to do?

"You should come out with me."

I shook my head. "I'm going to get started on my homework."

"You're always doing homework. Take a break."

"Really, I'm fine. I'm not much of a going-out kind of person."

"You are seriously repressed."

"Who is?" Cashien walked in, his pants tight enough they probably needed butter to get into, his T-shirt molded to his upper body. A man on the prowl for another man. He more than likely wouldn't be home tonight.

"Abby is staying home to do homework."

Cashien paused before stealing a chunk of brownie from the container on the counter and popping it into his mouth. "But it's Saturday."

"I tried to tell her that she was being seriously boring."

Boring was good. Especially since I lived in fear of their reaction when they heard who I was. Surely, they knew by now. And if they didn't, it was only a matter of time. They might respond better if the news came from me.

"Listen, you guys have been great with me, but I should warn you before you hear about it somewhere else... My parents—"

"Were never actually convicted of anything." Jag walked in with that bold statement.

"You know?" My tone hit a low note.

"That you're the daughter of the Pentagram Killers? Since day one," Cashien said.

My cheeks heated. "I was going to tell you."

"Tell us what? That your parents are famous? I also knew," Kalinda remarked. "Who could forget your face? That meme of you and the cops made you famous."

"But you never said anything."

She shrugged. "Why would I? You didn't kill those people."

"Neither did my parents," I exclaimed.

"If they're innocent, then I don't know why you're hiding." Kalinda sounded matter-of-fact.

"It's called being discreet," I mumbled. I went for the counter and the brownie I'd refused earlier. I needed something sweet, but Cashien had stolen the last cut piece.

Kalinda offered me a knife from the wooden block as I sighed at the treats in the pan.

Jag's grin widened. "Are you sure we should let the daughter of the unholy killers use a knife?"

I stiffened, Cashien snickered, and Kalinda looked as if she'd toss the blade at Jag's head. I kind of willed her to.

"She'd better not borrow my knives for any killings. They're mine," she snapped. Then gave me a glance. "But if you need something to pummel anyone with, you can use the hammer. No one's claimed it."

"I am not killing anyone," I hotly declared.

"Pity. It might have made you more interesting." Jag swept past me, and I glared at him.

"He's right," Kalinda said, catching my stare. "You're a college student in bed by ten. It's appalling."

"I read past midnight," was my feeble defense.

Cashien made a disparaging noise. "That's not something you should brag about."

"Nothing wrong with reading," I mumbled defensively.

"Screw that. I prefer to be doing," Jag declared, turning from the fridge with a beer in hand.

"What are you doing? I thought we were going out tonight," Kalinda declared.

"Still am. Just having one for the road." He winked. "Things to do. People to see."

They all had stuff happening, meaning by ten o'clock, the house was dead-silent. To prove a point, I ignored my bed and sat at my desk, studying. By eleven, I'd given up on homework.

I couldn't concentrate, not when I still mulled over the discovery that my roommates knew who I was and didn't appear to care. It honestly baffled me.

For one, why not mention it? Surely, they could have alluded to it in passing. Two, they had to be lying about not being bothered. Human nature practically ensured it preyed on them. The fact that they'd pretended not to know until now set off all kinds of alarms.

What if they were setting me up, Carrie-style? Could be they were spying on me, maybe with hidden cameras, feeding news of my every move to a public paying to watch it? The web was an ugly place with the worst kind of voyeurs.

The idea of being spied on had me pacing and searching the room, looking for stealthy video recorders and microphones. It wasn't that I was worried they'd see something. I was as boring as Kalinda claimed, but I deserved privacy.

By one a.m., I was still awake as if I'd chugged a vat of coffee. With my mind moving a mile a minute, I put on my running shoes and headphones and headed out for a jog.

Stupid, right? Women weren't supposed to go running alone at night. I read the damned articles about them going missing only to be found dead. I heard the lectures about how if women didn't want to be victims, they should stay safely inside.

It pissed me off. Sometimes, I wanted to run at night. Needed to feel the cold breeze on my skin, the darkness on my flesh. There was a certain heavy quiet that you could only experience at night, not the same as the predawn silence. That one trembled with pending wakefulness. But at night, you shivered with fear as the worst you could expect emerged to stalk.

I threw myself into a jog, figuring I'd play it safe and at least run inside the college campus on the well-lit paths. The campaign led by previous assault victims to make the area safer had borne fruit. Now, lights were strategically placed, and every few posts, cameras watched. Nothing could happen that they wouldn't see.

I went around the quad once, the initial burn fading into a pleasant warmth. I veered into a second lap, my earphones playing soothing ocean sounds. I couldn't hear my steps, just feel them, the soft pounding as the soles of my shoes hit the pavement.

The sudden grasp of my arm startled and had me acting. Reflexes honed by years of martial arts kicked in. I grabbed the offender and used my weight to flip them. They hit the ground with a satisfying *thud*.

13

THE PERSON WHO'D GRABBED ME *OOMPHED*, AND I knelt on a thick chest, digging in with my knee. I stared down at a familiar-looking face. "I know you," I said, not easing up on the pressure. The guy I'd pinned sat in a few of my classes.

He smiled lopsidedly at me. "I'm Erik. I've been trying to muster the courage to meet you. I'm a big fan. I've got a whole series of articles dedicated to you."

At his words, my lips pulled into a grimace. He was one of those freaks turned on by the media firestorm.

"I'm nobody special." I moved off him, and Erik scrambled to his feet.

"Not special? What are you talking about? You're the Slaughter Daughter. And your pics don't do you justice. You're even hotter in person." He licked his lips." What do you say we go somewhere?"

My nose wrinkled. "Ew. No." What was it with guys who thought I was some kind of slut?

"Then let me take some pictures, at least. Do you know how much I could make if you give me some titty shots?"

"This conversation is over." I went to move past him, but Erik reached out to grab me roughly.

"I didn't say you could leave."

I looked at the fingers clamped to my arm. "Let go."

He squeezed tighter. "You're coming with me. Maybe instead of pics, I'll take a video of us fucking. Me, fucking the daughter of serial killers." He practically panted with excitement.

"They were never convicted," I spat, jerking out of his hold.

He moved faster than expected. He lunged, and in moving backwards, I tripped over the edge of the path where it dropped into the grass. I hit the ground on my back, my head slamming hard enough that it left me dazed. The bright-eyed fucker landed atop me, pinning my hands by the wrists, using his weight to subdue me. I bucked.

"Get off!"

It only served to excite him. "You like it rough?"

I'd show him rough.

I struggled, and he murmured, "What's wrong with your eyes?" I managed to get an arm free. Before I could break his nose, someone cleared their throat. I looked sideways to see legs, leading up to a dark sneer.

A sneer I knew.

"Is this a one-man rape or can anyone join in?" Jag drawled.

A chill went through me. I wished I hadn't been a moron, jogging at night. What the fuck was I thinking?

"I saw her first." My attacker seemed to think he could call dibs.

"You are an asshole," I declared. Vastly irritated, I snapped my head forward and heard a satisfying crunch. I managed to shove Erik off and move away before the blood spurted. While he yelled and clutched his face, I rose and faced Jag, who stood with hands in pockets.

Would I have to fight him off next?

"He'll probably cry to the administration," Jag remarked as the wanna-be rapist stumbled to his feet and ran.

"It'd be dumb because then they'd know what he tried."

"His word against Slaughter Daughter's. You really think you'd win?"

I already knew the outcome and sighed. "Why is it so hard for people to leave me alone? I'm not like my parents."

"I thought they were innocent."

"They are."

"Then why wouldn't you want to be like them?"

I glared. "I am not in the mood to argue with you or deal with you twisting my words."

"You don't seem to be in the mood for much. Always studying. Never going out. Are you always this boring?" he asked.

"It's called taking my education seriously."

He snorted. "That's a bullshit answer, and you know it. You don't have to live like a nun to keep good grades."

You did with a nickname like mine. "Why do you care what I do?"

"I don't. Just find it curious that you never do anything at all."

"It's safer that way."

"Safety is overrated," he said, keeping pace with me as we headed for the house.

"I'm not boring," I blurted as the building came into sight.

He paused to eye me. "You're definitely not as expected."

"Meaning what?"

He shrugged. "You're just you."

"Was that supposed to be an insult?"

"Calm the fuck down and stop being so defensive all the time."

"Am not."

"Whatever. Don't go wandering by yourself. It's not safe," he said before walking away, leaving me to wonder if he would have helped rape me. Because he certainly hadn't done anything to save me. Not lifted one finger to protect me.

The fact that it even crossed my mind angered me because I wasn't a princess who needed a prince.

But the next day, I needed a hero.

14

I SAT IN THE DEAN'S OFFICE. THE WOMAN COULD have been as young as her forties, her skin smooth, but the iron in her hair and the steel in her gaze spoke of experience. She also appeared quite no-nonsense, meaning I had a bad feeling in the pit of my stomach.

"We had a complaint," Dean Dangerfield said, starting the conversation. "Assault on our campus grounds."

"So he admitted he attacked me first," I mumbled.

"That's not how Mr. Jerome recollects the incident. He claims you startled him when he was going for a walk."

"Lie," I hissed.

But she continued. "Mr. Jerome says you

waylaid him and became quite vocally aggressive about going somewhere with him. When he said no, you grabbed him. Given your background, he feared for his life and fought you off, suffering injury in the process."

I gaped. "That's not even close to the truth. He grabbed me. Said he wanted pictures. When I refused, threatened to rape me."

"Making false accusations is truly abhorrent. Mr. Jerome is a fine young man and an outstanding student."

"I'm not lying." The unfairness of it had me fighting hot tears of rage. Would my psychiatrist think my urge to slam the dean's face off my fist justified? I clasped my hands tightly and tucked them in my lap. After years of not being given a fair shake, I should have been used to it by now.

"I'm afraid our school policies are clear. You—"

"Sorry, I'm late." A guy entered without knocking, and I half rose to leave when he said, "Sit, Ms. Baker. It took me longer than expected to retrieve the video footage of the incident for your defense."

My what? I sat back down and stared at the guy with blond hair, long enough to be at home on a beach with a surfboard. It brushed his broad shoulders and the suit jacket he wore over a white button-down shirt. Despite the surfer-boy hair, his jaw was clean-shaven, square in shape, and his nose bumped as if it had been broken before.

"Mr. Mathews, I am not sure why you're barging into my office."

"I'd say it's fairly obvious: your appointment with Ms. Baker, which really should have come through the Student Advocate's office. The lack of notice barely gave us time to prepare, but luckily, we pulled enough information together to discuss the incident."

"There is nothing to discuss. Due to her actions, Ms. Baker will have to vacate the college premises."

Mathews shook his head and looked almost gleeful as he said, "Now, Mrs. Dangerfield, before you make yourself look foolish, perhaps we should play the evidence." He pulled out his phone and lay it flat on the desk. A simple press of his finger started the video.

It was a camera feed, and I recognized it immediately as the section of the pathway where I had been attacked. It showed me jogging past without incident. "Just a second, that's the first time she runs around," Mathews said and fast-forwarded until I came bouncing into view again.

It showed me with my head down, arms tucked, and then the lunge from the bushes as the student attacked me. It also showed how quickly I disarmed him, how he grabbed me once I let him go. The ensuing struggle where, for a second, my eyes glowed like those of an animal caught in headlights at night.

Weird.

I didn't see Jag in the footage, but it didn't matter. It showed that I was attacked. For the first time since I'd been called to the dean's office, I smiled.

Only to frown as Mrs. Dangerfield pursed her lips. "She broke his nose."

"In self-defense, after he grabbed her not once but twice." Mathews leaned over the desk. "Do you really want me to take this to the public? How quickly before they condemn you for encouraging a rape culture where male students aren't held accountable?"

"She's the daughter of serial killers." The real truth emerged on a hiss.

But my defender didn't back down. "Daughter of people accused and not convicted. Her parents have not been put on trial, and even if they were guilty, you are showing undue prejudice and revictimizing her simply because she's related to them. According to her transfer files, she's a hardworking student who was attacked on your campus. She should be demanding restitution for your negligence, along with Mr. Jerome's expulsion."

The dean gaped. "But his father—"

"Is rich. I know. Making Mr. Jerome's actions even more scandalous." Mathews shrugged. "But that's your problem. We'll expect a satisfactory resolution that includes an apology to Ms. Baker, or we will take this public."

"Sorry." The dean spat the word at me.

I wanted to dance on the dean's desk. I wanted to shout, "In your face, biatch!" Instead, I was mature and said, "Just a misunderstanding. And you don't have to expel him. I just want to be left alone."

"I can't control what the students do, Ms. Smith." She intentionally used my old name. "If I were you, I'd watch my step." The threat clearly indicated that she'd be watching me. Fair enough. I'd be watching, too.

I exited the office with Mathews and said, "Thank you, I—"

"Just doing my job." He strode off and didn't once look back. Almost as if he weren't happy to have helped.

Weird. But who cared? I'd just survived my first expulsion, and it was only the first month.

By the middle of the week, I kind of wished the dean *had* kicked me out. I lay flopped on my bed, face buried under pillows, bored out of my mind by my science homework. Dull stuff. Big words and meanings. I'd rather be playing with bodies.

Dead ones.

Hmm. That still didn't sound right.

I'd been so careful in choosing my courses so that people wouldn't catch on to my fascination with death. I was studying to be a forensic analyst and yet I'd have been happy as a mortician. The human body fascinated me, and even better, dead people didn't talk or move. I found them easier to relate to.

Rolling onto my back, I sighed. The house was quiet. More than likely the others had gone out. They did that a lot despite their classes.

While they often asked me to join them, they respected my wishes and left me alone. Kind of. No one bothered me when I was at home. Yet outside of it, someone was always around when I least expected it. I'd be sitting on the quad, eating the lunch I'd scrounged from the fridge, and I'd look up to see Cashien watching me. Other times, as I had to walk past a snickering bunch of students, they would go silent, and Jag would suddenly walk through them.

I made no friends but after the incident with the very rich Erik B. Jerome, I didn't seem to have acquired any new enemies. Life became respectably boring. And I hated it. Was even beginning to seriously think of saying "yes" the next time Kalinda asked me to join her at a club.

Someone rapped on my door and walked in before waiting for a reply.

I eyed Jag, the bane of my existence, who'd never come into my room before. "What do you want?"

"Cops are at the door looking to talk to you."

The instant he said it, I went through a myriad of feelings. First and foremost, fear. Had they come to arrest me?

I did the mature thing. I ducked my head, pretended to look at my textbook, and said, "I don't want to talk to them."

"Say no, and they'll probably come back with a warrant. Go see what they want."

I looked at him. "Excuse me, but have you dealt with cops before? More specifically, cops that think you're guilty of something?"

"What makes you think they're gonna blame you for anything?"

"Don't tell me you haven't gone online to see the thousands of theories about me."

"Are any of them true?"

"No." Not even close. At times, I could still be surprised by how sick some people truly were. And yet I'd bet they didn't have to deal with the bullshit I did on an almost daily basis.

"Then you've got nothing to worry about."

"I wouldn't have thought you so naïve."

"Not naïve, but not stupid either. I've dealt with cops before," he stated, pushing away from the doorway. "And I know for a fact that ignoring them won't make them go away."

I groaned at the ceiling. "I am so tired of this. Everywhere I go. Same shit. Different day."

"Whine later. Stall any longer, and things might get difficult."

I glared at him. "I don't like you right now."

"Hate me later. Let's go, buttercup."

Buttercup? The most ridiculous name. Yet I followed, grumbling, "I'd really rather study." I went down the steps and immediately saw two officers, well inside the house, the door gaping at their backs. All I could think of was my mom yelling at me not to let all the heat out.

The cops didn't seem to care that they might be taxing our heating and cooling unit. They stood with their feet slightly spread, hands dangling for one, in belt loops for the other. Their light tans spoke of their mixed heritage, while the glitter in their eyes reflected a hope that they'd have something exciting to share over donuts tomorrow—which I used to think was cliché. Wrong. It proved true. I'd spent quite a bit of time in police stations, and there was always a box kicking around. I used to eye it, but only some of the cops got the hint and offered me one.

Those that didn't made me wonder how much chaos would happen if I sprinkled a little bit of poison, the kind that would have them cramping and curling into balls of shrieking agony. I was sure my old shrink would tell me that was a normal reaction. I used to worry at times where he'd draw the line when it came to responsibility for a crime.

Not to mention, I would never use poison. It left traces and a body. The courses I took in college taught me plenty about forensics. Which probably only fueled the fire about me. But, to be honest, if I went into law, they'd assume it was to cover my ass or my parents'. Medical field? Obviously, honing my cutting skills. Biology? See medical. It didn't really matter what I did; someone would find a way to relate it back to the ugly rumors constantly plaguing my life.

Despite the urge to run back up the stairs, I made it to the bottom step before saying, "Hello, officers, my roommate says you want to talk with me?"

The portly male with the mustache addressed me. "I'm officer Walters. This is Officer Jenkins. You're Abigail Smith?"

Uh-oh, they'd used my old name. "Actually, it's Baker now. And I go by Abby. I'm trying to leave my past behind. New start and all." I saw no sympathy in their expressions.

"Where were you last night between the hours of midnight and two?" Walters asked, his mustache barely moving.

Despite feeling my blood turn icy cold, I managed to reply, "I was in bed. I had class today at eight."

"In bed. Meaning no alibi." Jenkins, his skin slightly pockmarked, sounded almost gleeful. He reached behind him, probably for his cuffs.

Apparently, I'd given the wrong answer.

"What's this about?" I'd forgotten about Jag. He'd remained slightly behind me, but now he slid into place at my side. Probably morbidly curious, and yet that didn't explain the oddity of his arm snaking around my waist. I might have elbowed him except... something told me to wait.

"Sir." Walters had his most serious mustache face on as he looped his fingers hard at his belt and puffed out his chest. "This doesn't concern you. We are asking Ms. Smith her whereabouts."

"And she told you. In bed. With me." He purred the words, and I just about visibly shivered. He'd given me an alibi. But why?

"Ms. Baker didn't mention you when we asked."

I hastened to jump in. "We don't like to advertise that we're sleeping together."

Jag's arm squeezed. "The house guardian frowns on fraternization."

Since when did we have a house guardian?

Who cared? He'd given me an alibi, and I milked it. I leaned in to him. He was as solid as he looked. Cold, though. His arm fit nicely around me, and his hand palmed my lower belly. Anxiety made me quiver. Nothing else.

Nope. Nothing. Else.

"We'll need someone to verify you were together." Jenkins wasn't letting his chance slip. He had the cuffs clenched in his fist. He wanted to use them, but he was smart enough to know that he needed a valid excuse.

Walters clung to what his partner demanded. "You'll have to provide a witness."

"Perhaps I'm just hard of hearing, but I could swear you just asked if we had someone watching us fuck," Jag said softly. "Maybe I should call for our other roommate. He's a law graduate. Top of his class, actually. I wonder what he'd say to your request."

I couldn't help but be blunt. "Do you have an audience when you screw your partner? Maybe you videotape it."

"You can't ask us that." Walters turned an interesting color.

Jenkins was the boor who actually said, "Did you videotape it?"

"No!" I yelled. "No one watched us having sex."

"Calm yourself, ma'am." Walters held out his hand. "We are just trying to confirm the truth."

Jag sneered. "By questioning our word."

"Because I think you're lying." Jenkins leaned in with a mean look in his eye. "I think you're covering for Ms. Smith."

"And I think you've got nothing," Jag taunted.

"What's going on?" Kalinda flounced from the kitchen area, wiping her hands on a dishtowel. "Why are there police officers in the house? Is this about those parking tickets? I have a court date to fight them." She tossed her head.

"We're here trying to ascertain Ms. Baker's whereabouts last night," Jenkins stated.

"She was here. In bed."

"Alone?" Walters asked.

Kalinda didn't once look at me or Jag. Couldn't have heard what he claimed. I wanted to groan as our story prepared to fall apart.

"No, she was not alone." Kalinda rolled her eyes. "You can tell she and Jag are still in the newbie phase of dating. They kept me up a good portion of last night with their frolicking."

"How can you be sure it was Ms. Smith?"

Kalinda's eyes glinted with humor as she said, "Because we share a bedroom wall." Only now did she turn to us. "If you must fornicate, you could at least move the bed away from the shared partition. The knocking is rather distracting." The rebuke had me gaping. For one, it was beautifully delivered. I would have believed her outrage if not for the fact that I slept alone.

The cops, though, had no reason to assume Kalinda was acting.

"I see." Walters' entire mustache drooped in disappointment.

Jenkins blustered. "Banging walls don't mean the suspect was on the other side."

I held my breath at the word. Suspect in what?

"Ain't no DA gonna touch an arrest without something more concrete," Walters remarked.

"Fuckin' pricks." Jenkins took his hand off his gun, something I'd only just noticed. I blamed my distraction on the situation—and maybe just a tiny bit on Jag's arm still looped around me, making me all too aware of him.

Walters didn't leave quite yet. "Have you spoken to or seen your parents recently?"

"What do my parents have to do with anything?"

"Just answer the question," Jenkins snapped.

"My parents are dead and have been for years." They abandoned me without explanation. I still had issues. My shrink told me that was normal. But he also seemed to think if they'd lived, I'd have forgiven them. Not without a pony, I wouldn't. I'd always wanted one, and they owed me.

"You came here thinking she might be a suspect. A suspect in what?" Jag asked.

"Has something happened?" Kalinda added.

Jenkins looked practically gleeful as he dropped the bombshell. "A pentagram was found drawn in the abandoned church by the cemetery. Forensics is running tests on the stains inside, but it's looking like blood. Human blood."

Fuck.

15

My mind blanked. I felt as if I were a stupid character in a shitty C horror flick. And then it hit me.

"You came here thinking I killed someone?" I gaped at the cops.

"You have to admit, it's suspicious," blustered Walters.

"Suspicious how? What evidence do you even have linking me to it?"

"It's a pentagram."

"And?" I prodded. "Pentagrams are a widely used symbol. Not to mention, my parents were never actually convicted of anything. And on that basis, you showed up here, ready to arrest me." I stood as tall as I could and said in my most victimized voice, "Is there absolutely no presumption of innocence anymore?" A shame no one recorded this. It would have been a viral sensation.

"You know what? This conversation is over. Next time you want to talk to my girlfriend, talk to her lawyer first." Jag shifted in the officers' direction as if he'd toss them out.

"Ms. Smith isn't under arrest."

"Yet," Jenkins added.

"This is harassment," Kalinda declared. "And victim intimidation. When was the last time you went through a sensitivity training course?"

"We're done here. Sorry to have bothered you." Walters seemed most put out. Jenkins sagged.

They left, and I practically hit the floor, a nearby wall the only thing holding up my sagging body.

Kalinda bolted the door and leaned on it long enough to say, "I think it's safe to say, we need a drink. Cocktails in the kitchen. Now."

If I had breath to protest, I might have. Instead, I followed her into the kitchen, parked my ass on a stool at the counter, and slouched. I didn't know what to say. My previous encounters with the cops were about giving them information about my parents. This assumption that I might be linked to a serious crime bothered me. If Jag hadn't been here, would they have really arrested me and thrown me in a jail cell?

"Drink. Tell me if it's sweet enough." A glass slid in front of me, the tan liquid in it bobbing with ice cubes. I'd wager it had alcohol.

I shook my head. "I can't."

"Stop being so uptight." Sexy, purring Jag had reverted to his usual sardonic self. "Have a few swigs and relax."

"I can't relax," was my miserable admission.

"Then they win," Kalinda said.

I put my face in my hands. "I can't believe this is happening. Why can't people just leave me alone?"

"The joys of fame."

My lips pursed. "Infamy, you mean. I could do without. Bad enough people are obsessed with my parents, but every time shit happens, someone assumes it's me. Because, you know, I must be some kind of psycho, too."

"Obviously. I mean, who eats Fruit Loops without milk?" Jag said from his spot leaning on the counter. He was no help.

I was mad at him, but not too mad. After all, he'd come to my rescue. By pretending we were lovers, he'd kept me out of the clink.

But that didn't mean he could disparage the way I ate my cereal. "I like them crunchy. And I wouldn't talk. You're the guy who eats French fries with plum sauce instead of ketchup or mayo."

"He is a savage," Kalinda agreed.

Cashien entered the room. "Any reason our address was given out on a police scanner?"

It didn't take long to catch him up.

He eyed me, and I waited for the condemnation. "They had no grounds to take you, and barely any to ask you questions. If they show up again, refuse to answer until I arrive."

"What if they plant evidence?" It happened all the time in books and movies.

"If they try framing you, then we get it tossed out." Cashien pointed. "What are we drinking?"

"Long Island iced tea," Kalinda replied. She reached for the glass she'd poured me and drank a few long pulls before offering it to Jag, who drank the rest.

Cashien protested. "Sharing is caring, bro."

"Not in this case. Didn't you say something about cutting back?"

"One-night stands, not booze," Cashien grumbled.

"Too much alcohol leads to the former. Besides, I did you a favor. Needs more sugar," Jag advised, pushing the glass at Kalinda.

"You're only saying that because you have a sweet tooth," Kalinda admonished, even as she dropped a spoonful of sugar into the pitcher and stirred. She ended up pulling out more glasses, and a moment later, everyone had their own, including me.

"What are we toasting?" Cashien asked, lifting his glass.

"To keeping Abby's ass out of prison and teaching her to lie better." Jag was as nice to me as ever.

"Hey," I protested. "I went along with your story."

"You need to work on your 'I had a great night of sex' facial reaction."

"I'm sorry. I had a hard time imagining you good at it," I snapped back, and Cashien just about fell off the stool laughing.

As for Jag, I expected him to look angry, and something hot *did* flare in his gaze, but it was more of a smolder than a snap. "Touché, buttercup. Perhaps a demonstration of my prowess can be arranged. Because next time, Kalinda might not be around to cover your lack of proper reply."

"How about we don't have a next time?"

"I'll drink to that." Cashien tilted his glass at me and then drank.

Jag and Kalinda followed suit. I looked at my glass with its amber liquid. I grabbed it and drank. It tasted like iced tea and yet it warmed me as it went down. I set the glass on the counter but kept my fingers curled around it. "I can't believe you're being so nice to me." I really couldn't.

"Why wouldn't we be nice to Abby?" Mary asked, walking into the kitchen. Within minutes, she knew the story too, and I drank some more iced tea and got a refill. The warm buzz kept me company as Mary hopped onto her laptop to find out what the cops had so far.

No one questioned the fact that she could actually find out.

"The nine-one-one phone call was made by someone walking their dog. Apparently, the dog ran inside an abandoned church. When the person went in after them, they saw the pentagram and called for help. The first officers on the scene noticed the suspicious stains and cordoned off the area for testing. Quick prelims show it is human blood."

"How old?" Jag questioned while I took another warm and fuzzy sip.

"The more extensive lab results haven't been posted yet." Mary kept tapping. "But the cemetery security guard did his rounds around ten-ish, and it wasn't there then. He didn't find it until his second pass."

"So, pentagram and blood. I've heard nothing in this story yet about a body." Cashien paid attention to the finer details.

"Nothing according to the report I'm sifting through." Was it only me who wondered how Mary got into the police computers? They all seemed to accept it as just something she did.

"No corpse is good. Hard to prove a crime," Cashien mused aloud.

"That's what you think." My parents were convicted in the court of social media despite never being arrested and charged." Never given a chance to prove their innocence.

"What are we going to do?" Jag asked.

There was no we. It was my problem. "I'll be moved out by the weekend." I couldn't stay here now. Didn't matter if the pentagram thing was a hoax. All eyes were on me, people waiting for me to screw up.

"You aren't going anywhere," Kalinda declared. "Whoever is behind that thing in the church just needs to be found."

"Then we can have a talk." Jag's smile was anything but nice, and yet it warmed me.

I didn't feel as despondent as usual, and I realized it had to do with the peeps sitting around me. "Why would you help me?"

"Because someone is screwing with you," Mary replied. "I mean, come on. I'm looking at this police report. It's bullshit. They did not have enough to accuse or arrest you." She shut the lid of her machine. "Arresting someone because of a coincidence? That's not right."

"Could someone be framing her?" Kalinda asked.

"A person with a grudge might." Jag eyed me. "Who hates you?"

"The world?" I offered with a useless shrug. I couldn't help but think of Erik and his obsession. How far would he go?

As if reading my mind, Jag said, "Could be that rich prick you punched. Might be revenge."

"Could be him, a copycat, or someone random." Cashien laid out the possibilities.

"In the meantime, until someone is caught, Abby will have to be careful lest someone decides that getting rid of her will cure the ills of the town." Kalinda gave me a worried glance.

"Maybe the perp left a trail. I'll look for any surveillance footage around the cemetery," Mary offered.

"Meanwhile, I'll have a chat with the fucker who attacked you last week. See if he's holding a grudge." Jag flashed a deadly grin.

"Wait, what? Someone attacked Abby?" Kalinda exclaimed.

Which resulted in another explanation,

including my retelling of how the dean had tried to kick me out of school but couldn't because the student advocate came to my rescue. By the time I finished my story, Kalinda was eyeing her knives. I wondered if she had the same drunken idea I'd had about performing a Bobbitt. People like Erik needed the kind of lesson they couldn't forget.

Apparently, violence was contagious. "The more I think of it, the more this seems like the kind of thing that sick fuck might do. I'm going to track him down." Jag shoved away from the counter.

"No hitting him," Cashien admonished. "You're already on probation."

"For what?" I asked.

"Nothing," Jag mumbled, slouching off.

Cashien also left, declaring he had some studying to do, which didn't explain his choice of skin-tight leather pants. Mary skulked off next, something about an online group event. Meaning it was just Kalinda and me. The silence stretched.

"I'm sorry," I ended up mumbling. "I knew this would happen. My past. My parents." I fluttered my hands.

"You didn't cause this." She cleared the counter of dishes, smoothly slipping them into the dishwasher.

"Maybe not, but the fact of the matter is I'll

never escape the rumors, and that's disruptive and unfair to you guys."

"You're not moving out," she stated, grabbing a dishcloth and wiping the granite surface.

"It would be best."

"For whom?" she asked, stopping in her tidying up to eye me. "You need us."

I didn't understand her insistence. "We're just roommates. It's not a big deal. I'll find another place."

"And then who will be your alibi the next time the men in blue come knocking?" She arched a brow.

"I can't have someone glued to my side twenty-four-seven." I pushed from the table and left, knowing I should be more grateful for their help. Instead, I was angry at them for being so nice. For being supportive.

Did they understand how much I wanted friends? Someone who believed me—believed *in* me? At the same time, I knew my supposed sins would tarnish anyone associated with me. Jag might have meant well coming to my defense, but he'd probably regret it later. As my alleged lover, the cops would now scrutinize him, as well.

Life could be so fucking unfair.

The alcohol gave me a nice, warm buzz, enough that the thought of going upstairs to my room didn't appeal. It was probably the height of stupidity to go walking by myself after the visit from the cops. What if someone's cat went missing? I'd become the number one suspect.

My shoulders hunched as I trudged, bypassing the campus's lit paths for the meandering roads of town. At this time of night, the lamp posts' fluorescent heads shone. There was little traffic, just the occasional car moving past me on the road, the faint *boom-boom-boom* of music a fading noise as they sped away.

I was on a quiet street with rows of townhouses, each sporting a single spot driveway, almost all of them with a car parked. The stoops in front of each home led to a door, all of them different, some with big windows, others solid and carved.

My feet slapped on the concrete sidewalk, and I kept my head down, hands shoved into my pockets. I heard the whisper of someone following.

Was I being stalked? Would I be mugged? Raped? Worse?

Not another soul around except for the footsteps behind me.

It occurred to me to whirl around and confront the person. Face my fear. What if I frightened myself for nothing and it was simply someone out for a walk, nothing harmful intended?

A door opened, spilling light onto a wooden stoop painted white—maybe gray, hard to tell in the low light. A figure moved down the steps, male and dressed in a jacket to go with pressed slacks. It wasn't until he hit the sidewalk and looked at me that I recognized him.

His name slipped from my lips. "Mr. Mathews." My savior from the dean's office.

He frowned, obviously not happy to see me again. Only his gaze went past me, and his eyes widened. "Behind you!"

A violent shove sent me flying. I managed to get my hands out to break my fall, the pavement digging and scraping at my palms, while my knees bruised at the hard impact. As I gasped at the pain, my hair hanging in my face, I heard the running steps and the shouted jeer. "Murdering cunt."

Tears pricked.

Mathews crouched in front of me. "Are you all right?"

I peered at Mathews through hanks of hair and managed through a tight throat, "Never better." Such a lie. All I wanted to do was cry. And that, in turn, made me angry. I should be chasing after the bastard who'd attacked me, smashing his face off the ground.

"Let's see those hands." He grabbed me by the wrists and didn't give me a choice but to rise and rock back on my haunches. He inspected my palms. "Those scrapes need to be cleaned."

"I'm fine." I snatched back my hands and pushed to my feet, unable to stop a grimace as my knees throbbed in protest. I took a step and winced.

"You are not fine. I'll give you a ride back to your dorm."

At the offer, I finally looked at him and his stony —hinting at pissed—expression. "I don't need your help. I said I was fine."

Something sparked in his gaze. "You're obviously not okay. Not to mention, you probably shouldn't be walking by yourself given what just happened."

That caused a hysterical giggle to bubble up and escape. "Do you really think this is the first time?" I'd been shoved into lockers, had rocks thrown at me, been spit on, threatened.

Maybe he had a point.

He raked his fingers through his hair. "Listen, I get you don't like me—"

I interrupted. "I never said I didn't like you, but it's pretty obvious you don't have a high opinion of *me*."

That brought a frown. "It's not that I don't like you."

I arched a brow. "Then what is it? What have I done to you?"

He stared for a second, then he sighed. "Nothing. Let's just chalk it up to me not being a people person."

"Aren't you the student advocate?"

"I don't need to like people to help them."

"Then it seems like an odd job choice."

"Not when it helps pay my tuition. Come on. Let's get you home." When he would have touched me, I jerked, and he froze before gesturing instead. "My ride is parked at the curb." He pointed at a nice car, two doors, sporty-looking. I couldn't have said what make or model. I didn't pay attention to those kinds of things, but the seat hugged my body when I sat.

Mathews slid into the driver seat and didn't say much as he pulled away from the curb. "Where to?"

I gave him the address, and silence fell. To my surprise, he broke it, but only to chastise me.

"Given what happened before, I would have thought you'd learned your lesson about going out alone at night."

My lips pinched. "It's not fair. A woman should be safe to walk by herself at any time of day."

"The world isn't a safe place to start with. Add in your past, and that only multiplies the danger for you."

"Meaning I deserve it?"

"I never said that. But that guy didn't attack because you're a woman. He did so because of who you are."

"And who is that exactly?" I replied, the words dripping with bitterness. "Because last I checked, I was a girl who thought her life was boring and normal until the cops showed up at her school. I'm the girl who has been bullied out of just about everywhere at this point. Who can't even walk down the street without being attacked for something I didn't do." I stopped my tirade, my chest heaving.

It took him a moment to reply. "I'm sorry."

I blinked and then looked at him. Mathews had stopped for a light and stared right back. He really had nice eyes.

"*Are* you sorry? Because, technically, you're just like the rest. You didn't want to defend me. You hated me on sight."

"I don't hate you. Although I will admit I might have let certain rumors color my view of you. But that doesn't mean you aren't entitled to justice. And you certainly don't deserve to be attacked."

"You shouldn't have bothered coming to my aid," I said with a sigh. "Now that the dean's been embarrassed, she'll be looking for any excuse to ditch me. And if she's the vindictive type, you might get caught up in my trouble."

The car rolled into motion again. "I can handle myself."

I snorted. "I thought I could, too. But life has a way of fucking with a person."

He parked the car by a curb outside a house I didn't recognize. "This isn't my place."

"It's mine. Since I'm not sure what you have on hand for first aid, I thought we'd make a pit stop and get your wounds taken care of."

"You don't have to help me. I'm okay." So long as I ignored the stinging and the fact that I'd have to dig tiny bits of gravel out of the wounds.

"Let me do this." His gaze remained intent. "My way of saying sorry for being a dick before."

It would be bitchy to refuse his apology. "Fine." If he was a psycho who wanted to hurt or kill me, he'd find himself surprised. Because I wouldn't go down without a fight.

He lived on the second floor of a converted triplex. I entered a modern space with more color than expected. White walls provided a stark backdrop for the vivid art. Bold slashes of color that changed almost as I moved into the space, the images within ever-changing.

The couch was white leather with bright cushions. The kitchen chrome and white marble, yet all the accoutrements were bright red.

"Sit. I'll get the first-aid kit." He waved to the couch, but I chose a chair. Let it be a subtle hint that while I might have entered, I wasn't looking to hook up.

He returned and said nothing as he laid the red box with its white cross on a chrome and glass table. He crouched on his haunches and reached for a hand, only to frown. "We should wash these out first." He tugged me to my feet, but rather than take me to the kitchen, he pulled me into a short hall with three doorways, two of them closed. We went into a large bathroom.

He turned on the water and stuck his hand under before indicating that I should rinse mine. The babying amused me because I seriously could have done this on my own. Just how inept did he think I was? Then again, he had seen what'd happened.

To the casual observer, I must have seemed pretty placid. It hid the inferno inside that wanted to scream and hit back.

The water stung my abraded skin. I hissed but kept my hands moving back and forth under the spray, seeing the blood and dirt rinse away until I had only scrape marks left.

He offered me a dark blue towel, part of the matching set he kept neatly folded on the bars.

I hoped this was a guest bathroom because no man should ever be this neat. Or a woman, for that matter. It was unnatural.

Once I'd patted dry, he inspected me again, his fingers more callused than expected.

"Looks like we've got all the dirt out," he stated. "Take off your pants, and we'll do your knees."

I laughed. "I don't believe it. You're using this as a creepy come-on line."

"What? No." His brows pulled together. "You tore your pants." He pointed to my leg. "I can see the blood."

I glanced down. My knees didn't look so good now that he mentioned it.

"I am not stripping to my thong." Too late, I realized what I'd admitted.

He did too and grinned. "While I'm sure you look amazing in your underwear, I'm really only trying to help. Can we roll up the legs?"

I nodded. The thin fabric of my leggings slid up easily enough until it got past my knee, then it started constricting my circulation, but my virtue remained intact. More or less.

He carefully dabbed at me with a washcloth, grumbling each time I winced. "Sorry."

"Not your fault," I said as I hissed.

"It was a dick move."

I didn't disagree.

When my wounds were clean to his satisfaction, we returned to the living room, where I sat in the chair once more. He dabbed at my scrapes with an antibacterial cream, but I drew the line at going to the hospital for stitches. I did agree to bandages and grimaced as I emerged, looking like a mummy. Not much choice, though, given my left knee kept bleeding. I'd have a nice scar once skirt season came around again. Great.

It felt odd to have a man kneeling in front of me. A man who didn't say much. A man I didn't know how I felt about. He'd admitted to disliking me. Apologized. Now, he tended me. It made a girl wonder what he intended next.

Apparently, nothing. As soon as he'd patched me up, we headed out the door to his car. I finally asked, "That house you came out of. Was that your girlfriend's?" Yeah, I was fishing.

"Friend." He said nothing more as he drove me home. To my surprise, he walked me to the door.

In front of the closed portal, I faced him and found myself oddly shy. "Thanks."

He stared at me, and I couldn't read his expression. I should have expected his brusque, "Try and stay out of trouble."

He walked away without a backwards glance. I

shrugged and entered the house. Thirsty, I grabbed water from the fridge. Jag came in the front door just as I was heading up the stairs. He looked annoyed and flushed.

"Whose car was that coming down the drive?"

"Mr. Mathews. I don't know his first name."

"You let a guy you don't know drive you home?" Jag's arms folded over his chest. Angry. Formidable. Sexy.

"Mathews isn't dangerous." Not like someone else I knew. I glanced down at his scraped knuckles. "What happened to you?"

"Nothing."

Lie. He'd done something. "Did you beat up Erik?"

"No."

He strode into the kitchen, and I followed. "Then who did you fight?"

"No one." He slammed open the fridge and grabbed a bottle of water.

"You're pissed."

He shot me a dark look. "No more than usual." It was then that he noticed my bandaged hands. "What happened?"

"Nothing. I fell," I lied.

He growled as he suddenly came at me, all tall,

bristling male, who bumped into me as he said again, "What happened?"

"Somebody thought I was taking up too much room on the sidewalk and shoved me. Not a big deal."

"Who?" His expression turned dark. "Did anyone see him?"

I rolled my shoulders. "No idea. And not worth finding out."

"They intentionally hurt you."

"Yeah." I didn't deny or defend.

He grabbed my wrists more gently than I would have expected. He lifted them and stared as if he could see through the bandages. His jaw tensed. He glowered. Then glanced at me. The intensity of his stare caught me. I swayed in his direction, and his eyelids dropped to half-mast. Sultry. Sexy.

Rather than kiss me as expected, he suddenly dropped my hands and strode off, taking the stairs two at a time. *Thump, thump, slam.* Someone was in a mood.

I, on the other hand, felt kind of good if I ignored the sting in my hands and knees.

The next day, I woke and went to class with a smile.

It didn't last long.

16

My day started out fine. A shower, then breakfast, which for me consisted of a dry bowl of cereal and a cup of coffee. Kalinda hated it and did her best to offer me her idea of a healthier start to my day: muffins, fruit yogurt. Ugh. On the weekends, she went all out with eggs and bacon, but I avoided the crowded kitchen and never got a taste.

I was checking emails when I heard Kalinda suck in a breath and begin cursing. Not in English, and it was seriously fantastic. Even pissed, she was absolutely stunning.

And then she narrowed that gaze on me and said, "You don't know."

"Know what?"

"A body was found last night."

"Do they know who it is?"

"Not yet. The face is mangled, so they're trying to find out if anyone is missing while they run fingerprints and sequence the DNA. They're also doing a campus rollcall."

"They think it's a student?" I shoveled another handful of cereal, enough that I wouldn't be able to talk if I wanted to. This couldn't be happening.

"No, but there are rumors."

"Oh? What kind?" Yeah, I played dumb. I wanted this to last a little longer. Wanted to pretend I could have had this life. I really liked Kalinda and the other peeps I lived with.

Kalinda snapped. "Don't play dumb. It's a dead body. Of course, people are saying you had something to do with it."

"I didn't kill anyone, but I get it. Perception is everything. I am, after all, Slaughter Daughter." My lips turned down as I indulged in an inner pity-fest. "I just need an hour to pack my stuff."

Kalinda stared at me. "What are you talking about? Why would you leave?"

"You just said people think I did it."

"Did you?"

"Of course, not!" My exclamation emerged hotly as I tried not to cry.

"Then I don't see the problem."

My voice wobbled. "The problem is, I'm going to

bring unwanted and negative attention to you and the others not only in this house but also on campus. Every wannabe reporter and blogger will start following me around, taking my picture, doing things to provoke me for a video. And it will happen to you, too. Because people are assholes." My mouth twisted. "I'll leave before there's any trouble."

"Oh, shut up. And don't be such a drama queen." Kalinda waved her hand. "We are not going to have you running away from the idiots. You did nothing."

I angled my phone at her and pointed to a trending hashtag. The meme wasn't flattering to the school or me.

Kalinda pursed her lips. "Social media is evil."

I totally agreed. "Worst thing ever invented." If only I'd been born in the seventies or eighties, I might have managed to be anonymous enough to make it through life. But in the twenty-first century, there was nowhere to hide. Everyone had a camera, it seemed.

To this day, I remained the opposite of photogenic. The memes had some extremely horrible images to work with. Like my grad photo with its unnatural smile and pose. Then there was a volleyball action shot from the yearbook with my hair pulled back, my face sweaty and flushed, grunting as I bumped the ball.

I'd changed my look since then. Didn't matter. Someone always outed me.

"We need a plan."

"It's called move away and lie low," I muttered.

Again, Kalinda dismissed my proposal. "Scurrying away will only make you appear guilty. I know you're innocent."

Amazing how much those words meant. "Innocence won't matter. With my parents dead, the cops are going to look for a way to pin this on me."

Kalinda wasn't deterred. "You have an alibi. How exciting. Jag as your lover."

I wished. "I don't want anyone lying for me."

"I'm not letting you get arrested. You're my friend, Abby. I look after my friends. And that's final." She cupped my cheeks, and I almost bawled my eyes out. It was seriously the sweetest thing. To be myself, in front of someone, and not be rejected.

"Thank you," I whispered.

"Thank me by moving your butt. Get dressed and be downstairs by eight-fifteen. I'll drop you off for class."

"I can't go to class!"

"You need to act as if everything is normal."

"Things aren't normal," I reminded her. Not to mention, I didn't want to sit through a class on the evils of social media. On the other hand, Mr. Santino might be the only person who could provide an oasis in the coming storm.

"Fake it until you make it. How do you think I get through the day?" Kalinda retorted.

"You? You're like super Miss Confident."

"And yet inside, I'm a mess of nerves. I'm just better at hiding it." She winked.

"I can't. If I go out there..." I hung my head. "It won't end well." I'd been in this exact situation twice before. The second time I left before it really escalated. And in those cases, there weren't any pentagrams or fresh bodies.

"You will be fine."

"Until they try and arrest me."

"On what grounds? If something happens, and they take you into custody, refuse to talk and ask for your lawyer."

"I don't have a lawyer." Although, I did have the savings to hire one if necessary.

Kalinda snorted. "Don't be an idiot. If you get in trouble, call me, Cashien, or Jag."

"Jag's not a lawyer."

"No, but he will make sure you get one."

Would he? "You're making me think I would be better off not going out."

"You can't hide, Abby. Get out there and hold your head high."

"Easy for you to say. You're not the one everyone is staring at."

A sly smile twisted her lips. "People stare at me, and I use it as empowerment. If they're negative, then I'm stronger. If they're jealous, it's because I am better. You can either fear the attention or feed on it."

Using a lot more words, she basically said what my last therapist had when talking about my mood. Control the narrative.

"This is going to suck," was the recurring phrase I repeated the moment I stepped out of the Jeep onto campus. Kalinda offered a jaunty wave before driving off, almost mowing down some students, then lowering her window to indulge in her sing-song version of road rage.

No one would ever call her Slaughter Daughter. She'd be the Lovely Widow or something equally cool.

Head ducked and wearing a baseball cap, I avoided detection as I headed for the lecture hall. It didn't stop me from hearing the excited whispers. *"Did you hear?"* And snippets of salacious detail. A body drained of blood. One group of people were convinced that the fingerprints had been burned off, too.

I also heard my nickname. I hunched my shoulders as I passed a group of freaking co-eds extorting people to sign the petition to have Slaughter Daughter expelled from the college to keep them all safe.

Nothing like being innocent but declared guilty by the mob. The pariah bit was getting old, though. Why should I suffer listening to them? I'd done nothing wrong. Yet look how they treated me.

As I entered the lecture hall and headed down the stairs, those already there recognized me. My cheeks burned as I heard them conversing with hushed excitement. When I hazarded a glance to my side, other students stared, not bothering to hide their fascinated revulsion.

These strangers judged me even as not one had ever spoken to me. Must be nice to feel so superior. I wanted to scream in their faces. Hack into the college server and screw with their grades.

I would do nothing. My shrink would be so proud.

I slumped in my seat, having chosen front row middle, as close as I could get to my teacher. Looking for protection? Fuck, yeah. Would I get it? That remained to be seen.

Mr. Santino arrived at nine on the dot. The class chattered as he placed his satchel on the table at the front.

He stood and waited, but his students couldn't seem to control themselves. Rather than curb their morbid curiosity or temper their cruelty as they speculated about my parents and me within earshot, they got louder. Someone even shouted, "Ask her. Ask where the blood is."

Kalinda was wrong. I should have hidden. Was it too late to run?

Bang.

The strident sound of a heavy book being slammed on a desk shut people up, and in that sudden quiet, Mr. Santino very succinctly said, "Everyone currently and intentionally being cruel to a classmate by propagating inflammatory speculation get out."

No one moved.

Mr. Santino tucked his hands behind his back. "I didn't take everyone in this room for liars."

A brave one spoke up. "You can't kick us out for talking about current events."

"I can for bullying, though. You're Theodore Baskin. Correct?

"Yeah."

Mr. Santino activated the lecture projector, and a social media profile appeared on the screen. The round avatar was of a young guy, curly blond hair, wearing a striped shirt. Name: Theo "Long Arm" Baskin.

"Is this you?" the professor asked, tucking his hands behind his back and turning to glance at someone in the higher seats.

"Uh. Yeah. But I didn't give you permission to show it," Baskin complained.

"I don't need permission since your profile is public. As is your feed. Shall we see what you like to post?"

The first meme was my grad photo, but instead of holding a diploma, someone had photoshopped in a knife. The caption was: *Getting my degree in psycho.* I heard a few titters.

The next two posts didn't cast me in a flattering light either. More laughter erupted, louder this time. I wanted to turn into a puddle and sink into the nearest crack in the floor. This was humiliating.

Santino found my gaze and held it. Held it and didn't laugh. Oddly enough, his stare comforted, soothed, seemed to say that everything would be okay. *Trust me.*

I didn't have much choice.

The room kept murmuring and laughing but hushed when Santino flipped to a true-or-false slide.

"How many of you believe all of those memes to be true?"

I heard rustling but had no idea how many hands rose.

Mr. Santino told me. "Five. How many think these are funny?"

I could feel the discomfort and noticed Mr. Santino's arched brow as he said, "Come on. Fess up. We all heard the laughter."

Uncomfortable shifting had Mr. Santino then counting aloud. "...Twelve. Thirteen. And despite not holding up your hand, that includes you, Mr. Baskin."

"Come on," Baskin whined. "It's a joke. It's not like I believe that shit or anything."

"It's cruel, false, and you knew that but still posted it," Mr. Santino pointed out.

"I didn't make it. I just shared it." Baskin launched his defense.

"And it's funny," someone else added.

The professor eyed me once more and then asked softly, "Ms. Baker, are you amused?"

Shit. Why did he have to bring me into this? "No," I whispered, the word barely there, but everyone heard.

People who feel shame for their actions often attack, so I wasn't surprised when someone blurted, "Who cares if the memes are true or not? We all know she shouldn't be here. Fact is, she's the daughter of the Pentagram Killers. And now look what's happened."

"Ah, Mr. Anthony, you raise an interesting point. Especially your claim of facts. Let us examine them, shall we?" It was as if my teacher had planned today's lesson around me and the mess on campus because with a flick of his finger on his phone, he pulled up my past and projected it onto the screen.

It began with a newspaper report, the headline bold:

Pentagram Killers Strike Again.

"For those who aren't familiar with this case, more than two decades ago, pentagrams began appearing, etched into basement floors, some undiscovered for long periods of time given their location in abandoned buildings. They were considered remarkably unique, given the shapes were burned into the floor. Right into cement in some cases. Within those grooved lines, investigators around the country found dried blood. Human blood. Enough that it was unlikely the person who donated survived."

The word used in my time was *sacrifice*.

Mr. Santino moved to the next article, and I winced.

Pentagram Killers Caught in the Act.

My teacher resumed his lecture. "A video that

was never sourced surfaced, appearing to show two people identified as Mr. and Mrs. Smith."

"Killers like in that movie," someone in the crowd shouted. As if that were the first time I'd heard that joke.

"Except the video never showed them killing anyone." He hit play. I would have hidden my face, but he caught my gaze. It would be okay.

Just as brutal as ever. I was surprised that he dared to show it.

When it ended, he put a question up on the screen. *What are the facts?*

A student, her voice high-pitched and excited, exclaimed, "They killed someone by draining them of blood."

"I saw no knife," the professor pointed out.

"There's a body."

"A body-like shape," he corrected. "That crime scene and supposed body were never found."

"Come on. You know they killed someone. The man had his hands in the blood," another student piped up.

"And? Do we know it was real?"

"They identified the guy." Baskin was back.

"Yeah, I heard he killed his boss," Anthony added.

Santino was prepared as he riposted right back.

"Mr. Smith's co-worker died, yes. But they never had any evidence as to who killed him. So, a body with no evidence, and a low-resolution video."

"You can see their faces. How can that not be proof?" Baskin argued.

"I'm glad you asked." The next slide was a collage of pictures featuring Theodore Baskin in a variety of scenarios: a face screaming in protest, holding a gun, doing all kinds of stuff.

"What the fuck is that?" Baskin yelped. "I didn't do any of that shit."

"It's proof, according to you."

"It's fake."

"Exactly. And here's the thing, that video people used to condemn the Smiths? It was never sourced. No one ever saw the original or discovered who filmed it. Someone could have altered the faces." The on-screen image changed. The hooded person in the video was now wearing Santino's face, then a series of faces. Judging by the gasps and angry exclamations, the people depicted belonged to this class.

With each fake the professor showed, I felt better. But the fun and games stopped as he went back to my case. "So now that I've shown that the video isn't worth shit, let us now move on to the rest of the facts. We have no bodies. No missing persons."

"The guy on that video is missing."

"The problem being, they never found a body."

"Probably a homeless person."

"Can you prove it?" Santino retorted.

"There was human blood in the pentagrams," Baskin countered.

"Could have come from a blood bank."

A feminine voice spoke up next, sweet with a hint of slyness. "Why did her parents run if they were innocent?"

And there it was. The logic everyone always came back to. Innocent people didn't run.

Innocent people didn't abandon their daughter and go on the lam, only to end up dying in a car accident thousands of miles away.

"Have you ever been unjustly accused of something, Ms. Larimer?"

I was impressed at how he knew everyone's name.

"If someone accused me, I'd argue my case. And win," exclaimed Ms. Larimer. "I'd win because I'd have the truth on my side."

I arched a brow at her snippy reply. My teacher wasn't about to be taken down by the likes of her. "The truth can be manipulated. Emotions, especially emotional blackmail, can be very persuasive. It's all about the spin."

I shouldn't have been surprised that he had a

slide for Ms. Larimer. The meme showed two versions. Pretty and perky, smiling in a selfie, then the ugly—getting out of a car while spewing puke. Labeled simply: before and after.

Ms. Larimer took offense. "That is repulsive and false."

"Prove it."

"I don't have to prove it because it never happened."

Santino pounced on her words. "Prove it. Prove that's not you in the picture."

"I don't know why you're harassing me. This is not the same. I'm not a drunken slag. She, though, is Slaughter Daughter."

"Which means what exactly? She's automatically guilty? No due process? You would accuse her and post vile things—" He began throwing them up onto the screen, screenshots of comments and memes and who posted them. When he stopped, the screen was filled. "And that's just a portion of it. It's not okay. What you post has consequences. The things you find amusing, the rumors you spread, cause harm. Keep in mind that, oftentimes, even the news headlines, stories, and images aren't about the truth but evoking an emotion. A reaction. Clicks. Likes. Advertising revenue. But there are consequences for callousness and bullying."

The professor then flipped to more headlines. But after the first, I had to duck my head because once I saw the word *suicide*, I fell into a dark place. A reminder of the thoughts I'd battled when everything happened. The despair that threatened to swamp me when it felt as if it were me against the whole world.

In many ways, it was.

The post drew comments from some of the students, even an apology from a girl who said she knew better given someone had bullied her online.

I didn't face any of them. I had no interest in apologies. I just wanted to be left alone. Despite being uncomfortable for most of the class, I felt drained and stayed behind at the end of it. The professor ignored me until the last student exited and then turned his gaze on me.

I held it. Chin up. I wouldn't let him intimidate me.

His lips curved. He was a handsome man. No ring on his finger, but that didn't mean shit.

"Did you have a question, Ms. Baker?" He used my new name.

"Did it ever occur to you to ask me before using me as part of your lesson?"

"Given recent circumstances? No." He didn't

apologize, leaving me with a choice. Stomp as I left or discuss things.

There was also a third option. "For a person who teaches about social media, you have absolutely no online presence." I'd gone looking.

He leaned against his desk, a good six to eight feet between us, and yet it felt intimate. "I'm online. I'm just cautious about it." A good-looking guy, I could see why he didn't offer private meetings. Knowing what I did after years of college, I'd bet he got propositioned a lot, and not for better grades.

"I had to get off all the chat platforms." I stuck only to actual news sources, not opinion rags where the clicks and ad revenue drove the slant of their stories. I never posted my picture online. Ignored all the swirling internet urban legends about my parents and me. It hurt to read and hear from people who claimed to have seen them. I just wished they'd let it go.

"But you monitor the stories." Stated, not asked.

My shoulders rolled. "I can't exactly ignore them."

"Because the pentagram killings are still an unsolved mystery."

I rolled my eyes. "Not according to that updated mockumentary that came out." Amazing how facts could be whittled to form a narrative.

"I'm surprised they didn't put you in it."

"They would have if they could have, but I said no." More like the film crew came knocking, and I dodged. I knew whatever I said would be twisted into whatever they wanted.

"Not tempted to tell your story?"

I snorted. "They'll call me a liar if it doesn't fit their view of what happened."

"What did happen, Ms. Baker?"

"I don't know. The only thing I can be sure of is that I didn't kill anyone."

But the cops appeared convinced that I had, and I could admit, I was starting to get the urge.

17

Mr. Santino might have opened the minds of those present in his class. Outside that room, the court of opinion had finished its session and rendered its verdict: guilty.

As I headed for the campus donut shop, I noticed the stares, heard the whispers. I did my best to ignore the wide berth around me everywhere I went. Not all teachers were on the same level as Mr. Santino. He at least understood what I was going through.

In my ethics class, Mr. Guillaume glared at me enough that it encouraged the soft murmurs to become loud catcalls. I left. Bravery didn't have to come with masochism.

I chose to skip the rest of the day. By the time I got to the house, I'd made my decision. I went straight in the door and up those stairs to my room so I could pack.

It was time I gave up the college dream. I'd finish by correspondence, or not at all. I had enough money to start over somewhere social media hadn't completely penetrated. Or at least not an American scandal like mine. Might even be time to move continents.

With it being the middle of the day, most of my roommates were in class. Good. Kalinda would probably try and talk me out of leaving again. She meant well, but she didn't understand how having me around could fuck up her life. If the copycat killings continued, I'd be strung up, convicted without ever having given evidence in a trial by my peers. Anyone associated with me would be tarnished by the same brush. It had cost me my only friend in college. We'd bonded on day one, but when I was outed two years later, Roxanne turned on me. Threw me to the mob.

That'd hurt.

If the people who knew you best could make false accusations, who could you trust?

Certainly not my housemates. I'd known them for less than a month.

I exited my room with my knapsack over one shoulder. The house was quiet. Too quiet. I winced at every perceived creak as I made my way downstairs. Everyone was probably gone, and yet, I kept expecting to hear someone question what I was doing.

Only once I slipped outside did I ease out a heavy breath. I'd been so certain that someone would stop me. Disappointment warred with relief at the fact that no one had.

I headed down the steps, having decided to walk a few blocks before hailing a ride via app. Two blocks and one turn later, I stood outside a coffee shop, latte in hand, waiting for my ride. I sucked at the froth as I spotted the motorcycle coming up the street, carrying a familiar helmet-headed form. Shit.

I turned and faced the shop. He wouldn't have seen me. Even if he had, he wouldn't stop.

Jag stopped. Over the rumble of the engine, he said, "Get on."

"Can't. Just got this." I held up my latte as I whirled to offer a false smile.

Jag lifted the visor on his helmet and straddled his bike. "Toss it and get your ass on."

"I paid six dollars for this. I'm drinking it. Besides, there's my ride." A small blue car pulled to the curb.

"You want to be arrested in that piece of shit or maybe avoid the cops a while longer?"

I stiffened at the question. "What are you talking about?"

"Mary overheard some chatter on the radio."

"What kind of chatter?" I asked, my tone wooden as I dumped my latte and approached.

"The kind that said they identified the dead body as Erik Jerome."

My stomach dropped. This wasn't happening. I wanted to scream my frustration. Kick something. Run. Could my being framed be more obvious?

"Fuck," I exclaimed. Then quickly added, "It wasn't me."

"The cops think otherwise. They're looking to bring you in for questioning."

"I thought we already gave them an alibi?"

"For the pentagram. Erik's murder hasn't been linked to it yet."

"Where else would the blood have come from?"

He shrugged. "Until they run the tests, they'll treat them as separate crimes, nullifying our alibi."

"If they don't match, I'm screwed." I bit my lip.

"Don't be sure. Someone witnessed me punching him."

That drew my gaze to his battered knuckles. "You hit him? Why?"

"Because I don't like assholes who attack women."

Jag's sexy level went off the charts. "Thank you."

Being Jag, he had to be a dick. "It had nothing to do with you."

Except he'd done it after my encounter with Erik. He'd saved me the other night with the cops, and he was coming to my rescue again.

"Me doth think you protest too much." I did a very bad quote of something gothic.

He grimaced. "I think you are wasting time. Get on the fucking bike."

"To go where?"

"You'll see."

Not the most comforting words, and yet my leg went over the seat, planting my crotch on the tiny wedge that was left. I had to wrap myself anaconda-style around Jag, my arms around his waist, my cheek on his back. He didn't have a spare helmet. I tried not to imagine my brains on the pavement when he took off.

It was more fun than expected once I realized I wouldn't immediately die. I even opened my eyes at one point to watch the streaming streets. We were going farther than the house. Right outside of town as it turned out. Jag turned into an old neighborhood, the type with massive open yards and mansion-style homes. He pulled in front of one with a roundabout driveway that could have fit a dozen or more cars.

"Whose place is this?" I asked, staring at the majestic manor. Old red brick, white shutters, too many windows to quickly count.

"It's your uncle's place."

I blinked. "I don't have an uncle."

"According to recently uncovered records, you do. Your father's bastard younger brother."

As I slipped off the bike, I turned to frown at Jag. "My father didn't have a brother."

"He does now. Mary's been working on creating a backstory online."

"You're really going to have to explain why I need a fake uncle. Because it makes no sense." Why would someone with money want to go through the trouble? Unless...

"Is this some kind of weird fetish thing? Have you sold me to a perv?" I backed from Jag as he removed his helmet.

"Are you on fucking drugs? 'Course not. Why would you even—?" His expression was almost comical as he grasped it. "People do that?"

I didn't reply.

"I'm not a sick fuck. I would never."

"You expect me to trust you?"

"Why not? I've never done a damned thing to hurt you."

"Yet. It's just a matter of time." It was always

only a matter of time.

"For fuck's sake, buttercup, I'm not that much of an asshole."

"Says you. People tend to have a change of heart when the tabloids dangle dollars in front of them."

His jaw worked as he swung his leg over the bike, placing his helmet on the seat. "Ain't no one buying me. And I'm not a rat. I'd never fuck you or anyone over like that."

"Why should I believe you?"

He moved into my space and looked down at me. "Because I would never hurt you."

"I would." I slammed my fist into his gut. Might as well have hit a wall.

He grunted. "Not nice, considering I'm trying to help."

"You shouldn't. It won't end well for you."

"Threats?" He pulled me close enough that I thought he might kiss me.

"More like reality. People get pissed when you abet a supposed killer." My lopsided smile hid the tightness in my throat.

"You're no killer. I would know," was his reply.

Before I could ask what he meant, the door to the house opened, and Professor Santino stood in the opening. He scowled at us before saying, "Get inside. Quick. We don't have much time."

18

"You? You're supposed to be my uncle?" I eyed my professor in his T-shirt and chinos. He filled them out nicely and looked about a decade too young to be related to me.

"According to the backstory we've created online, your grandfather never knew a one-night stand he indulged in resulted in me." Professor Santino winked. "As part of an experiment, I submitted to a few of those DNA places. Lo and behold, I found family."

"Why the fuck would you lie about being related to me?" I exclaimed.

"I'll explain shortly. Jag needs to get out of here so I can get you up to speed." The professor stood aside, an invitation to get my butt inside, but I glanced at Jag.

"Shouldn't we stick together?" I hadn't forgotten about the fact that he'd slugged Erik for me.

He offered a lopsided smile. "I'll be good. I'll do my best to slow down the cops so you can get your stories straight." Jag straddled his bike and gunned it, leaving me stranded with my new—hot—uncle.

"Let's get inside."

I blinked at the professor. "Please tell me the explanation comes with booze." Because I needed a shot of something stiff.

"Given we'll soon be dealing with law enforcement and the media, you should remain clearheaded."

"I know," I grumbled as I stepped past him into his house, "but I think I deserve a break. *Uncle.*"

"I agree. Hence why we put the cover story in place. Given we'll be spending a lot of time together, we needed to ensure I wouldn't be accused of inappropriate relations with a student."

"And why will we be spending time together?"

He offered me a wicked, very un-uncle-like smile. "Because you're interesting, Abby."

"You want to use me?" I stood in his front hall with its gleaming wood floors, a table in the middle of it with a vase of flowers.

"Very much so." He made it sound dirty.

"Doing what?"

I expected some kind of perverted demand and did a bit of a double-take when he said, "I am going to write a book about your experience."

"No."

"Why not?"

"Because my life isn't entertainment."

"It will make money. Lots of it that you'll get a portion of."

I snorted. "If I wanted dollars, I'd write it myself. It's more that I'm not interested in being dissected by asshole strangers."

"What if I told you this book will exonerate your parents?"

That froze me. Filled me with such hope, I almost killed him. "You're just saying that to get me to cooperate."

He shrugged. "I don't need your cooperation. I don't even need you to write this book. But I'd like to see justice."

"Why?"

"Because even if we never met, he was my brother. And you're my niece." He put a hand to his chest and looked so sincere, I gaped.

Then laughed. "That was some epic acting."

"We should be ready in our parts when the police come."

"How is having you as my suddenly discovered

uncle supposed to help keep me out of jail?"

"Because I won't let you get railroaded by bureaucracy."

"You realize having me around will bring scrutiny on you."

"Yes. And I plan to document all of it."

Did he truly grasp what he'd willingly invited into his life? I'd warned him. I'd done my duty. "How will you clear my parents' names?"

"By finding the real killer, of course. Because if your parents are dead, then it stands to reason this new Pentagram Killer is either a fake, or the true killer was never caught and has now resurfaced."

"Why start again? They were free."

"Because people who kill can't help themselves. Eventually, the urge becomes too strong. And I suspect your resurfacing might have been a catalyst. What better cover for new crimes than the daughter of those accused before?"

I wanted to refute his logic, and yet he offered an explanation. Maybe this was the chance I'd been waiting for to finally clear my name.

"Let's get you settled into a room before the cops get here. If questioned, you spent last night under my roof."

"If the cops ask Kalinda and the others, they'll know it's a lie."

"Already taken care of."

"You're making them lie?"

"Not exactly. They suggested it."

I grimaced. "I can't believe you'd do this. Pretend to be related to my family. I've done what I could to disassociate myself."

"And how has that worked for you?"

"Not great," I had to admit.

"Then time to try something new."

I followed him to a second floor down a hall.

"How many people live here?" Because the house was huge.

"Just me. And now you. I have staff maintaining the place, so if you need anything, hit the star on the room intercom."

"Being a professor pays, I see."

"Being a professor who writes books does."

"You're an actual author?" My fake uncle had suddenly gotten cooler. I frowned. "I've looked you up and never saw any books published."

"Because I write under pen names. My crime fiction tends to skew very adult." He winked over his shoulder. Definitely not an uncle wink.

Nor even a teacher.

And my next thoughts were wildly inappropriate as he flung open a door. "I hope this is adequate."

I gazed upon the cream and light blue room.

"Were you expecting a princess?" Because the opulence was astonishing. Thick, lush rugs over hardwood. A massive king-sized bed with pillows of all sorts. An oversized window with a cushioned seat, the bottom full of books. A fireplace flanked by deep chairs. A dresser topped with a basket of treats. I could see marble through an open door.

"There are toiletries in the bathroom. More clothes arriving before the end of the day."

"This is too generous, Professor," I declared.

"First, call me Joseph. Second, having you here is more than enough payment if that makes you feel better."

His ulterior motive actually did help because I understood why he acted.

"When should we expect the police?"

"Given they'll go after your known address first? Hours. Your roommates all have a busy day today. Meaning it will take the police a while before they track them—and then you—down."

It took them until dinner, which was chicken and sauce that had me groaning.

The professor's phone pinged. "It's time."

"For what?"

"Remember, say nothing unless you have to."

He'd given me pointers over dinner. What to say, what I could hold back.

My ice cream melted over my brownie as the seconds ticked by and stretched. I grew restless.

Santino eyed me sternly. "Hold it together."

When the knock finally came, I almost screamed.

"If you'll excuse me." He put his napkin on the table and rose to go answer. I heard the murmur of voices, then his loudly spoken, "Abby, we have company."

My turn to stand and toss my napkin onto the table. I pretended surprise as the professor—shit, Joseph...that would take some getting used to—walked in ahead of my two favorite cops.

My mustached friend Walters was back. "Again? What is it now?" I didn't have to feign annoyance. "I thought we already ascertained the fact that I have an alibi for your stupid drawing."

"We're not here about the pentagram. Someone's been murdered."

"And, of course, you thought of me," was my sassy reply.

Jenkins, who remained silent, dropped a hand to his gun.

My new uncle noticed. "You will not do violence in my home, officer. Keep in mind, I have cameras watching, and my niece is offering no threat."

"Niece?" Jenkins snorted. "That's a load of bullshit."

"The DNA doesn't lie, detective."

"No, it doesn't. Which is why, despite missing its head, we know the body found on campus grounds this morning was that of Erik Jerome."

"Ouch. Sucks to be him."

"Abby!" my fake uncle admonished.

"I'm not going to pretend I'm sorry that twat-waffle died. He wasn't nice."

"So you admit to hating him?" Walters pounced.

"I totally hated him. A hundred percent. But I didn't kill him."

"Going to lie and say you were with Jag again? We know he's your accomplice." Jenkins really had the bad-cop routine down pat.

"Officers, are these kinds of accusations neces-sary?" Joseph smiled and spread his hands.

"They are when we've got Slaughter Daughter on campus. It came to our attention that you and the victim had an altercation," Walters stated.

"You mean the video where he attacked me?" I made it clear.

Walters cleared his throat. "You defended your-self quite capably. Might have wanted revenge."

"I managed to escape only because he was distracted. He outweighed me. I don't know how you figure I'd have the strength to actually overpower him."

"Because you had help. You lured Mr. Jerome away so your lover could kill him."

I blinked at him. "Are you on drugs?"

Santino cleared his throat. "What my niece means to say is that your theory is baseless, and you know it. While you're trying to cram square evidence into round holes, the real killer is out there, probably planning his next kill."

"Want to bet if we lock her up, no one else dies?" Jenkins rocked on his feet. You could tell he was itching to handcuff someone.

"I think I've heard enough. Leave." The professor crossed his arms.

"Not until we ask Ms. Baker where she was last night," Walters insisted.

"Here with me. Having a family reunion," fake uncle said with a smirk.

"What time did she leave?" Walters asked.

"She didn't. Given the late hour, my niece spent the night. And before you ask, my security system was armed. She couldn't have left without my noticing."

Jenkins wasn't about to let me go that easily. "Maybe she knows your code."

"The system wasn't disarmed until I rose this morning. And I don't like your tone."

"This is a murder investigation."

"You should investigate people without alibis, then. Now, unless you're arresting someone, leave. And from here on out, if you want to speak to me or my niece, you'll go through our lawyer first." My fake uncle put on a cold and haughty expression worthy of royalty.

I wanted to stick out my tongue and give the cops a fuck-you middle finger. Instead, I reached for my untouched glass of water and chugged it. It did nothing to cool the hot anxiety within.

Apparently, my alibi was enough to keep me free for the moment. The professor saw them out and then returned to find me collapsed in my chair, eyeing the puddle of ice cream around my treat.

"What an unpleasant pair."

"They're just doing their jobs," I said dully.

"They're biased and close-minded."

"I agree. What can I do, though? Even I have to admit, given the circumstances, it makes sense they're targeting me."

"Which is strange in and of itself. Why would someone want to frame you?"

"What makes you so sure it's a frame job?"

"Because I know you didn't make that pentagram."

"How can you be so sure?" I asked.

"Because I know who did."

19

"WHO MADE THE PENTAGRAM?" I HALF-expected Santino to tell me it was him. I even worried he'd try to claim that it was my dad, back from the dead. I'd seen that theory floated around, given that only my mom's body was ever recovered.

His answer surprised. "Erik Jerome made the pentagram."

The very idea that someone would do something so heinous had me exclaiming, "How is that possible? He's dead. You're telling me he created it, slit his wrists, bled out, and then wandered off to be found days later?"

"Don't be foolish. He created the pentagram before his death—and not as cleanly as the ones from previous records. He was also sloppy with the blood.

Left the bags he'd stolen tossed in the woods behind the cemetery."

"Hold on a second. Erik stole blood to put in a pentagram he made?"

Joseph nodded.

"Nobody died?"

"Not in that pentagram, no. But Mr. Jerome is quite dead. It won't be long before the authorities are back with more questions."

"Or go after Jag since he used Erik's face as a punching bag," I muttered.

"Don't worry about Jag."

"Why? What are you planning?"

The professor wouldn't reply. "Get some rest. The next few days will be busy."

To spite him, and every other asshole who thought I was a killer, I almost packed my things and left. Curiosity kept me in the room I'd been loaned.

Could Santino do as he claimed and clear my parents? Which would, in turn, clear me. Or would his elaborate charade backfire? What would happen to me, to him, to Jag if the cops ever found out the men had been lying on my behalf?

I didn't have the kind of mindset that thought money and fame worth that kind of danger. It almost felt as if there were something deeper to the situation. Something I just couldn't see. But what?

I spent some time pacing my princess suite, then lying on the ridiculous bed. Given the turmoil, I'd thought sleep would be impossible, but the next thing I knew, I was drooling on a gazillion-thread-count pillowcase until someone yanked open the curtains and pulled back the covers.

"Ack! The light!" I made a sign against evil and buried my head under the pillow. Not very mature, I could admit, but it suited my mood. Which wasn't as black as expected.

How could it be with the sun shining and Kalinda trilling, "Move those lazy cheeks."

Pulling my head out from under my pillow, I fixed her with a bleary eye. "What are you doing here?"

Then again, what was *I* doing here? Yesterday seemed like some weird dream. A fucked-up reality no one would ever believe.

"I can't believe you had a hot uncle and never told me," she huffed.

I blinked. "Um."

Kalinda laughed. "Gods, your face. You bought that just as much as the cops did. Walters and Jenkins—sounds like a comedy duo."

"Don't even talk to me about them. They were here last night making threats."

"They'll be back. The news just reported that

Erik wasn't killed in the pentagram and have moved the date of his death to the day before yesterday."

"Which kills my alibi with Jag." I closed my eyes. "Guess I should get a last shower and meal in before they show up."

"Don't tell me you're just going to hand yourself over."

"What else should I do?" I asked.

"Not run away like you were planning. I can't believe you were going to leave without saying a word. Good thing Jag was keeping an eye on you."

"He was spying on me?" It explained how he'd tracked me down so quickly. "Why?"

"Because we were worried about you."

"Again, why?" All this sudden loyalty felt very strange to me.

Very. Strange.

Kalinda pursed her lips as she went through my half-strewn pile of clothes. "Because we're friends, and friends help each other out."

"They give each other rides and share clothes, not alibis for murder."

"Good friends do all that and bring a shovel to bury the body."

"You? Dig a hole?" I snorted.

"Maybe you don't know me as well as you think,"

179

she challenged, tossing me a shirt and pants. "Get dressed. We have work to do. Places to be."

"Maybe you do, but I don't. I am dropping out of college."

"To do what?"

I shrugged. "Dunno. I'll figure it out after I leave town." Change my name. Cut and die my hair. I'd go into hiding until the furor died down.

"Leave? That will make you look guilty."

I snorted. "And if I stay and more people turn up dead, that will prove my innocence? If I'm gone, maybe it will stop."

She sniffed. "That's the coward's route."

"What else can I do?"

"How about not let some jerk ruin your life? Stay and fight."

"Fight how? I have no idea who would be trying to frame me." The most likely suspect had turned up dead. "Besides, I don't think the cops are interested in looking at any other options. They want a tidy solution, which means finding a way to pin this on me."

"Except we're not going to allow it." Kalinda sounded so sure of herself. I wasn't as convinced.

"It's not a question of allowing. The cops have all the resources. All I have is the feeble truth, which is...I didn't do it."

"Then we'll have to make them believe you by finding evidence to prove without a doubt that these incidences are the work of someone else."

"But who? It could be anybody." Not to mention, Erik's death might not even have anything to do with me. Perhaps he had a gambling or drug debt. Maybe the town had blood-sucking vampire bats.

"We'll have to make a list of suspects. We'll start with your enemies."

"Could be a long list if we count all the online trolls who said I should have died with my parents."

"Then we best get started. Get dressed. I'm going to whip up some breakfast."

"I am not in the mood for breakfast."

She fixed me with her dark stare. "You are eating breakfast. We have a busy day ahead. Be downstairs in ten minutes." She exited the room, and I sighed.

It really would be easier to just leave, but given Kalinda's bossy nature, I wouldn't put it past her to hunt me down and drag me back by the ear like she'd done to Peter when he'd left a mess in her kitchen.

Despite her ten-minute warning, I took longer and showered, letting the hot water scorch my skin. I exited in a cloud of steam and toweled my body briskly before tossing the damp cloth over the bathroom door. I was standing naked in the middle of my room, underwear in hand, when someone flung open the door.

My eyes widened, and so did Jag's.

"What the fuck?" I squeaked. "Ever hear of knocking?"

Rather than apologize, he blamed me for the intrusion. "You didn't come downstairs." He continued staring. Not at my face—his gaze strayed lower.

I was only human and attracted to him, even if he was an ass, which meant my nipples hardened. He noticed, and I fought the urge to cover myself. So what if he looked at my naked body? A body was a body. He'd seen tons, I was sure. Yet I couldn't stop my skin from flushing. And that tingle between my legs? Not the right time or place, but that didn't stop it from happening.

"Because I'm a few minutes late, you think you can barge right in?"

"I thought you left," he repeated.

"Am I a prisoner who now has her every move watched?" I replied, giving him my back. I still had my underpants in hand and slid them on, conscious of how I had to bend to pull them up my legs and cover my butt. I expected him to leave. It would have been the polite thing to do.

"Someone has to keep an eye on you, given the trouble you keep getting into."

"What trouble? No matter what people think, I haven't done shit." I snared a sports bra from the pile and went to put it on. It got stuck, rolled up around my armpits, and refused to come down. My frustration burned, and yet I froze when I felt his fingers on my skin.

"Hold still for a second while I untangle it." He untwisted the straps, and I managed to cover my breasts. I flipped around to see him standing close. Too close.

I had to tilt my head to look at his face. He stared at me. And then he was kissing me.

His lips were on mine, and mine on his, and it was hot. So very hot. And passionate—his hands on my bare back. He grabbed and squeezed my ass, grinding against me. I somehow hit the wall, and with it bracing me, lifted my leg around his waist, spreading myself to him, getting the pressure of him where I needed it most.

His mouth teased mine. His hand slipped between our bodies to stroke me. He caught a soft cry and fingered me again, stroking me and bringing me quickly, but not fast enough that our lack of appearance wasn't noticed.

My intercom came to life with Peter groaning,

"Are you guys coming down? Kalinda is holding the food hostage again."

At the intrusion, Jag sprang away from me as if I were on fire.

It hurt. He'd been the one to kiss me. Touch me. He could have been a little less stiff as he said, "Don't take too long getting dressed. The gang is hungry."

"Why is everyone here?"

Rather than reply, Jag fled. I put my fingers to my tingling lips.

Jag wanted me. I was okay with that.

I finished dressing, brushed my teeth, and ponytailed my wet hair. Just in case I needed to move quickly, I stuffed my shit into my bag. My slim wallet with cards and cash went into my sweater pocket, my phone in my pants. I could abandon my clothes if necessary.

Going downstairs, I heard several voices. I eyed the front entrance, wondering if I should flee now.

Curiosity drove me into the kitchen to find the professor having a conversation with Cashien and Peter. Mary puttered on her laptop. Kalinda flipped stacks of pancakes. We were only missing Jackson and—

"Took you long enough. I was about to come looking for you again." His voice hit me from behind, and I whirled a little too fast. When I wobbled, Jag grabbed me around the waist and steadied me.

"Stop sneaking up on me."

"Not happening." He leaned in close to whisper, "Sometimes, you see amazing things when you least expect it."

The blush erupted, and I couldn't take it back. I broke my gaze with him and turned to look at the kitchen, an elegant space with a Mediterranean feel. The backsplash was beige stone, the cabinets a dark wood with a vine pattern etched into them. The appliances were all gleaming stainless steel.

The gang was mostly clustered around a large kitchen table set with eight chairs. They'd obviously noticed my arrival but didn't make a big deal about it.

"Why is everyone here?" I asked.

"Why do you think?" Jag moved around me. "Say hello to the team of Operation Save Slaughter Daughter."

I winced at the name, then grimaced as everyone looked at me.

"The lady we've been waiting for," Peter announced. "Now, can we finally fucking eat?"

Kalinda waved her flipper at him. "Yes. But you better leave some bacon for everyone."

"Yes, Mother," Peter sassed. He took only four slices and six pancakes. The stack was high, though.

Kalinda had also cut up some oranges, sliced some strawberries, and set out a bowl of whipped cream.

I had my first breakfast-gasm. Apparently, I'd been missing out with my measly coffee and dry cereal. The conversation flowed over me, and I absorbed the bits I thought most important.

"The body has already been taken to the morgue," Mary remarked, having taken a corner spot at the table so she could keep her laptop open.

The professor mostly had fruit on his plate and a tall glass of something frothy and pink. "I have a friend who works there. I might be able to finagle a visit."

I scrunched my nose. "Why?" I mean, the idea of going didn't bother me; I just saw no purpose in it.

"Because we need to see the body, of course. We have questions that need answers."

I frowned at the professor. "He's dead and missing his blood. How is he supposed to answer?"

"Don't you watch CSI?" Jag grumbled. He'd opted for coffee only. Probably explained his grumpiness. He should try a pancake orgasm with whipped cream and berries.

"Before we dive into the whole fascinating concept of forensics and dead bodies, I want to know what's going on." I leaned back from the table.

"Breakfast," Kalinda quipped.

"I do believe Abby is speaking of how I took on the role of uncle and the rest of you as her defenders."

At my nod, everyone stared at me. "I don't get it. I mean, no offense, but I barely know any of you. Why are you risking yourselves for me?"

"Hardly any risk," Jag noted, finally reaching for a piece of toast.

"You're lying to the authorities," I pointed out.

"Only to ensure they look in the right direction instead of the most sensational," Kalinda remarked.

"Legally, what we've done so far are only misdemeanors," Cashien added.

"It's above and beyond what you should do for a stranger."

"You're our friend." Mary lifted her head. "Friends don't let friends go to jail for crimes they didn't commit."

"How are you all so certain I didn't?" I let my gaze touch each of theirs. "I have no alibi. I was in bed at the time. Alone."

"You didn't do it." The professor sounded certain and looked more relaxed than I was used to. Which made me wonder how they were all here instead of in class.

"Shouldn't you all be on campus?"

"Given the location of the crime scene and the

shock, classes have been suspended for the next week," the professor informed.

"And for some people, the semester," Jag uttered in a low tone.

"What's he talking about?" I asked.

Santino replied, "The dean received a complaint about some of my subject matter."

"She's also pissed you're suddenly related to Abby," Jag added in a low tone.

"Dean Dangerfield has asked me to take a short leave of absence."

"You got fired?" Already my curse spread.

"It's fine. I was going on sabbatical to write your book anyhow. This just saves me from filing the paperwork."

"It's not fine. None of you seem to grasp that this is only the beginning. Helping me will screw you." I thrust myself out of my seat and aimed for the front door. When Jag moved to step into my path, the professor intercepted him with a low, "I'll handle this."

Except I didn't want to be handled. I wanted to be far away from people before they got caught up in anything. Only Joseph wasn't about to let his cash ticket walk out the door. He grabbed me by the arm, and I found myself steered into a study. He shut the door, giving us privacy. Not that I worried about being alone with him. If he wanted to assault me, he'd had the best chance the night before—or if I was going to be technical, during the wee hours of the morning.

Bookshelves lined the wall, and only a single window allowed light into the space. The ceiling sconce and scattered lamps remained dark.

The professor didn't sit, nor did he offer me a seat. He leaned against a desk strewn with books and paper.

"You can't run away."

"Why the fuck not?" I exclaimed. "What will staying do, other than have me accused of every bad thing happening in town?" I knew this for a fact because it'd happened before. Was it any wonder I felt an affinity for the Salem Witches? Both unjustly accused with facts twisted to suit.

"You need to drop the martyr act."

"It's not an act. I care what happens to others."

"We are all adults. We can make our own choices."

"Helping someone with my reputation takes away your choices. You got fired. What's next? Kalinda and the others expelled? Maybe implicated by the police?"

"I thought you wanted answers."

"Not at the expense of others, *Uncle*." I emphasized

the word and shook my head. "I still don't grasp what possessed you to fake a relation to me. You do realize when the cops find out, it's going to cause shit, right?"

A faint smile hovered around his lips. "Except they won't find out. The evidence we're related will convince them."

"Unless they dig deep," I insisted. "What if they demand another blood test and run it through their labs?"

"They won't, but even if they do, they'll walk away convinced of our relationship." He sounded so sure.

A pity I couldn't share that certainty. "How will we convince them? We look nothing alike."

"And?"

"You do realize a DNA test will quickly show it to be a lie."

"Will it?" he taunted. "If it makes you feel better, I've already arranged a paper trail that will withstand most scrutiny."

I stared at him, wishing I understood his true motives. How strange that this man, one with no relation to me, appeared so determined to protect me. And here I spurned him, even though he'd done more for me of late than my parents had. "

I moved to the window and stared at the front

yard, the green grass, stately trees, and planned flowerbeds. "This won't end well," I predicted.

"Why did you come here?" he asked suddenly.

"To get a degree."

"Obviously. But why here specifically?"

It occurred to me to lie, and yet, after everything he'd done, didn't I owe him something? "My mom grew up not far from here. Planned to go to this college, as a matter of fact."

"But didn't."

I shook my head. "She met my dad and moved to another state instead."

"You're doing this to be closer to her."

Was I? I shrugged. "Not really. I mean, she never even attended one class at this school."

The professor had moved without me hearing, and I only realized he stood close behind me when he spoke. "It's normal to miss the things you can't have." He put his hands on my shoulders and, for a moment, I thought of my dad.

Santino was nothing like him.

"I wouldn't know normal," I said with a high-pitched laugh, moving away. And then for some reason, I was crying. The hug felt both familiar and strange as my professor soothed me.

"Don't cry for that bastard."

Despite my earlier words, I sobbed, "He's dead." I pushed away and scrubbed at my face.

"Mr. Jerome was a stain on society. The killer did the world a favor." The professor sneered, and for a moment...just a moment...I could have sworn his eyes glowed.

"While Erik was a jerk, he didn't deserve to die."

"It is inconvenient given the scrutiny being placed on you."

"Inconvenient is someone using the washer and dryer when I need it. I'm the prime suspect in a murder case."

"Not for long." He sounded smug.

"Professor—"

He halted me. "You shouldn't call me that."

"Then what should I call you?" I sassed.

"Uncle is fine. Although I would wager you'd be more comfortable using my first name. Joseph."

"You told us never to use your name."

"The students may not, but your situation is different, wouldn't you say?" Again with the teasing smile.

"They will figure out we're not related."

"Doubtful."

"We know nothing about each other," I exclaimed.

"Which is understandable given our recent reunion."

"Prof—Joseph, this is nuts. You're risking your career. For what? I'm not worth it." Low, miserable words. If my parents didn't think me important enough to take me with them, why would anyone else value me?

"Ah, but that's where you are wrong. I think you're very special."

"I—" The words caught in my throat as he brushed my hair behind my ear. Again, something my dad used to do. But my dad was dead.

My query emerged huskily. "Do you have any clues as to who killed Erik?"

"A few theories, but I don't want to say until I know for sure."

"You have a suspect?" I whirled from the bookcase and its old, leather-bound books to glare at my teacher. "Who?"

"I need more proof."

"I won't say anything."

"Yes, you would, because it's human nature."

"By keeping quiet, you're protecting a murderer," I hotly declared.

"What if I'm wrong, though? It would ruin him."

Him. With one pronoun, he'd narrowed it down

to about half the people in the world. "What if he kills again while you dilly-dally?"

"What if he's killed during apprehension by the police, and no one ever looks deeper to see if he truly was at fault?"

The reminder of my parents' case snapped my mouth shut. No one had cared once my parents were ruled dead because the killing had stopped. Halted the minute they started running, as a matter of fact.

"What if something happens to you before you tell someone?" I argued for the sake of arguing.

"I won't give a name until I am one hundred percent sure."

"You're asking me to put a lot of faith in you."

"The question is, do you have faith in your parents?"

"They're not murderers."

Again, his eyes flashed. There one second, gone the next. "The evidence says otherwise."

"It's circumstantial."

"It's damning, and you know it. Not to mention, innocent people don't disappear and abandon their only daughter." He only repeated what I'd often thought myself.

"The system is unfair."

"Only if the evidence is stacked against you. We both know criminals with good lawyers walk every day. The evidence was flimsy. There was no DNA or fingerprints to put them at any of the possible crime scenes. No bodies, just blood—and it could have come from anywhere. A lawyer would have argued and gotten the case tossed had your parents stood for trial. The video would have been proven fake. They would have walked free and probably fled with you to start over."

My lips turned into hard lines. "Way to remind me how everything got fucked." Why hadn't my parents stayed to fight?

"Did you ever wonder if perhaps the police had irrefutable evidence tying your parents to the crimes?"

"I know the case inside and out." I'd studied every bit of it.

"Are you sure of that? Because it's not uncommon for some information to be withheld in order to ensure they can weed out false confessions."

"I thought you were supposed to prove their innocence," I huffed, pushing away from the bookshelf, my steps angry as I neared the professor.

"I can't be blind to the facts along the way. I'd like to prove them innocent, as it would then be a grand coup to showcase our justice system's inadequacies. But at the same time, if they are guilty..."

"Why would they kill anyone?"

"What are the usual reasons?"

"Money? My parents might not have been rich, but they did all right." Or so I assumed. I wasn't given everything I wanted, but I got two shopping sprees with Mom twice a year for clothes. At Christmas, I always had a pile of presents under the tree. While I didn't own a car, my dad had taught me to drive and never had a problem loaning me his Beemer.

"Ritual murders aren't about money. They're about power. And belief."

"I thought you were a professor of social media."

"Society in general fascinates me."

"With an emphasis on serial killers." I recalled the titles of the books sitting on the shelf in the bedroom he'd loaned me. Murder mysteries by two authors. One dark and violent, the other offering a sexy vibe to go with the shadowy danger. Both authors, though, had a thing for psychos. It hit me suddenly. "You wrote those books in the bedroom."

"I told you I was an author." He rolled his shoulders.

In my ignorance, I'd assumed a professor would have done something dry like a textbook, not fiction with covers depicting either spooky locales or a man displaying an impressive physique, holding a gun. It occurred to me that Joseph might not be a bad choice for setting a narrative. What did I want people to remember about me? How could we change the perception?

"Let's say for one second that my parents did make those pentagrams using stolen blood. Why? They were atheists. They didn't believe in God or the devil."

"What if the pentagram was about doing magic?"

I rolled my eyes. "My dad would not be doing magic." My dad wouldn't even cut our lawn in a checkerboard pattern. Still, there were those candles...

"Can you say that for sure?"

"Yeah, because magic isn't real." Or the death curses I'd aimed in the direction of some truly vile people would have taken effect.

"You are very rigid in your thinking. You'll end up overlooking possibilities as a result."

"If I want to believe that my dead parents weren't psycho, knife-wielding killers, then that's my prerogative. Maybe I don't really want to know what happened," I exclaimed.

"You do.

"Fine. I do. But I have a good reason. It's my parents. If someone framed them, they deserve justice. But you!" I jabbed my finger at him. "You're doing it for fame and fortune."

"Do my motives matter?" He crossed his arms over his chest, propping himself on the desk.

"Yes. I won't be a tool used and then tossed aside."

"Then leave." He gestured to the door. "Walk out. Go. Read about the truth in the paper once I solve the mystery."

"You can't solve it without me," I hastened to say.

"Why not?" He arched a brow.

He had a point. I offered nothing. "Good luck solving it." I waved as I grabbed the doorknob.

"If you leave, the cops will think it's an admission of guilt."

"I see it more as they can't pin anything else on me."

"Don't you want to know who's doing it?" He changed his tactic.

Much as I wanted to say no, that would be a lie. I wanted to nail the prick screwing with me to a wall. With real spikes. And a gag. Screaming would draw attention.

"Can't wait to hear the spin when it hits the news."

"If we catch the person. What if,"—Joseph pushed away from the desk—"the person doing this follows you? Starts it again in a new city, leading law enforcement right to you? Who will be your alibi then?"

The idea that someone would follow me wasn't any crazier than the fact they'd killed someone. The weight of the shit in my life hit me, and I sagged. Literally. Every ounce of courage holding me up just disappeared.

My ass hit a chair, and I kept slouching until my face practically touched my knees.

I didn't cry. I had no tears left, but I shuddered. Wondered when it would end. Started to think it might never.

The professor—Joseph—knelt and put a hand partially on my knee and hand. His voice was low. Soothing. "I didn't say that to crush you but to appeal to your fighting spirit."

I lifted my head to show him listless eyes. "I've been fighting for years. When does it end? Maybe I should just turn myself in." At least in a cell, I might get some time to study and not worry about a knock on a door.

"Let them arrest you. Fine idea," he said, springing to his feet. He paced as he expounded on my suggestion. "We can call them right now. News-papers, too. We want to make this flashy. The media will love covering the trial of Slaughter Daughter." I winced, but he wasn't done. "They'll start talking about the death penalty. Your face will be plastered everywhere. What a brilliant idea," he exclaimed.

"You're really annoying."

"So are you," he snorted. "Now, are you going to work with me on devising constructive ways to draw the killer out into the open, or whine?"

"That's your plan? Bait the real killer so they show themselves?"

"How else will they be arrested, and you exonerated?"

"What makes you think they'll kill again? Maybe it was a one and done." I poked a hole in his idea.

"Mr. Jerome wasn't shot. He was incapacitated and his blood drained. Not one drop to be found. Think about it." My teacher waited.

It took my slow brain a second to gasp. "The police are going to find another blood-filled pentagram."

20

PANIC FILLED ME. "I NEED TO LEAVE BEFORE THE cops find another bloody pentagram." They'd blame me for sure.

"You run, and they'll issue a warrant that will probably end in you being shot as they apprehend you."

"Geez, don't sugarcoat it or anything."

He pushed from the desk and got close enough to me that I could smell his aftershave. "I'm not going to coddle you because we both know you can handle it. You're tough. But you're also vulnerable. And stubborn. Stop arguing and listen. And maybe, just maybe, you'll get your life back."

"And if I don't?" I asked.

"Then with fifteen percent of the proceeds from the book, you'll do okay."

I rolled my eyes. "If you're any good."

"Oh, I'm good." He moved to the door of his office. "We've wasted enough time catering to your insecurities and abandonment issues. We should return to the others and set out some plans."

"My abandonment issues?" It emerged a little shrill. "Listen here, Professor—"

"Ah. Ah. Ah." He wagged a finger at me." What's my name?"

My gaze narrowed. "So sorry, Uncle Joe. It's hard to remember sometimes that I have an *older*,"— yes, I emphasized it—"family member in my life now."

"Old?" His turn to grumble.

It felt good to return the smirk. "Let me know if we need to take a break so you can have a nap." I flounced, not something I'd done often in my life, but when leaving someone speechless—especially a good-looking, arrogant ass of a man who deserved it— you should always have a little extra oomph in your step.

Kitchen cleanup had already been done. Jag sulked at the table, messing with his phone. Peter appeared to be missing again, probably avoiding the dishtowel Cashien wielded while Kalinda washed and handed over the non-dishwasher-safe items.

Mary still fiddled on her laptop but beckoned me over.

"What's up?" I asked.

"Give me your phone." She held out a hand.

I handed it over and asked, "What are you doing?"

"Turning on location services," Mary explained, thumbing through the menus.

"Won't that kill my battery?"

"Dead battery or more proof you weren't near crime scenes. You choose," she said, handing it back.

"Touché."

"Speaking of crime scenes, the cops are heading to a new one."

My dread trebled, especially since I glanced at Joseph, and he mouthed, *"Told you so."*

"Is it another body?"

"Yes, but that's not all."

"Let me guess, blood-filled pentagram. Where?"

Mary had the goods. "B building, first floor, room 103. The night guard was doing rounds and saw light coming from a crack under the door. When he opened it, he startled someone, who knocked down a candle as they fled. The guard chose to call for help with the fire rather than give chase.

"Please. If it was Percy, then he didn't chase

because he would have probably dropped dead of a heart attack," Jag mumbled.

"That's rude," Mary said hotly.

"But true," Jag retorted. "I'll bet the only time that man ever ran was because he heard the ice cream truck coming."

Mary bit her lip. Cruel humor, the kind you hated to enjoy. "Anyhow, the person making the pentagram fled. The fire from the candles took out most of the evidence and burned the body."

"Someone died?" Not another body.

She nodded. "Cops are hoping for enough DNA to figure out who it is."

"What about the person the guard saw? Was he able to describe them?"

"Persons. And not according to the police report." Something Mary had somehow gotten a copy of and had up on her screen. She pointed. "He says he saw movement only, no faces, no description other than they wore black robes with hoods."

"Of course, they were wearing robes," I muttered. Then something else struck me. "Wait, *they*? As in two?"

"Yeah, Percy claims there might have been two people there."

"Might?" I couldn't help but question.

"He never clearly saw the second person, just

movement hinting that whoever it was might not have been alone."

"Being so useless is really a spectacular feat," Jag retorted. "He couldn't even put out a few candles?"

"Fire is scary," I said in the guard's defense.

"It also destroys everything. They were covering their tracks," was Mary's observation.

I shook my head. "If they wanted to cover their tracks, they would have done it somewhere more discreet. This sounds like they wanted attention."

"Buttercup's right. They wanted to be seen. Wanted the scene to be found. Probably the same folks who murdered that douchebag, Jerome." Jag stood, the chair legs making a *skree* noise as they slid across the tile.

"You shouldn't talk shit about the dead." Mary's nose wrinkled.

"I will because he was a dick. And I will spit on his body when I see it later today."

"What?" I squeaked.

"Keep up, buttercup. I am going to ogle a dead man."

"But why? Wouldn't it be easier to read the autopsy report?"

The professor interjected. "If they've made up their minds, they might not be looking for anything that doesn't fit."

"They'll never let you near the body," I protested.

Jag tilted his head to my new uncle. "Prof's got a friend at the ME's office who says the place will be pretty much empty from two until four because of a staff party for someone's retirement."

"I'll go with you. To help." I tried to stay cool. But inside, I was kind of excited. A dead body. What secrets did it hide?

"No. It's not safe for you." Jag was blunt. "You should stay here or in public places, so you have an alibi."

Live my life under a watchful lens? "What's option two?"

"There is no other option." the professor stated. "Given the frame job, it's important you are not alone at any time."

"Even when I'm sleeping?" I asked with a sarcastic lilt.

"Especially when you're sleeping."

I almost asked if someone planned to share my bed to make sure my alibi was ironclad, but with Jag standing there, I kept it to myself. "I don't want my every breath and muscle twitch catalogued twenty-four-seven."

"Only for a few days. Weeks at the most."

Until we found who was doing this.

21

I was still moping when Jag and my new uncle left. Peter, Cashien, and Jackson were off doing whatever, so it was just us girls with an armload of hair dye.

"I'm thinking of going blue on top with a white undercut," Mary declared. "What about you, Abby?"

"Me? I probably shouldn't." With my luck, the cops would arrive in the middle of it.

"If you're worried about the police, don't. Cashien has already dealt with them and provided your alibi." Kalinda answered.

"He did? What alibi?"

"He was with you, studying." Said by my friend with a tilt of an eyebrow.

"Jenkins will accuse me of being an even bigger whore."

EVE LANGLAIS

Kalinda blinked. "That man is vile."

I shrugged. "In his defense, he thinks I'm sleeping with Jag, saw me with Mathews, and now Cashien is claiming he spent time with me." Which made me wonder why Cashien and not Jag...

"Lucky girl!" Kalinda winked. "All the more reason to play with your hair. Choose a color." She grabbed a box of purple. "I'm going for a long, chunky streak."

My currently plain brown hair hung over my shoulder. Mary didn't have a box of my natural auburn color, but she did have a hot pink. "Do you have bleach?"

She did. Soon, the smell of chemicals had us opening windows. Our hair was in aluminum foil as we prepared it for color.

We sat on kitchen stools, and Kalinda slid a jug of juice in front of us with a plate of cookies.

I almost choked when Mary mused aloud, "Do you think the pentagram in the school was made with Erik's blood?"

"Doubtful, given it already had a body," Kalinda pointed out.

For some reason, I felt a need to divulge. "The professor thinks there's another pentagram out there with Erik's blood." A morbid thing to even contemplate.

"He's probably right. Why else drain his body?" Kalinda sounded so matter-of-fact.

"Who does that?" I exclaimed. I was very happy that neither of them said my parents.

Mary bit her lower lip. "Blood magic is common in many cultures."

"But once you add in the pentagrams, the scope narrows." I would know, I'd done the research. "It's most likely a Satan-worship thing. Maybe we should be looking for a local cult."

"Satanists are not the only ones who like to do blood rituals and sacrifice."

"Come on, how many more clues do you need? Dark candles. Blood. Death. The inverted pentagram. The dark robes," I argued. I couldn't have said why I was determined to make this out to be some satanic cult thing. The *why* didn't matter, so long as we figured out the *who*.

"Robes don't mean shit. Someone might choose to wear a robe while killing for many reasons. For one, it's an easy garment to remove after blood spatter." Mary ticked off her fingers. "Ritual dress. Camouflage." More fingers lifted. "Could be the guard was mistaken, and he didn't see a robe at all."

"Leaving us with nothing usable," was my reply.

"Not exactly." Mary pointed to her laptop screen. "Interesting thing about the first pentagram found. The lines weren't even, and the grooves were too shallow, leading to the blood puddling outside them. Also, the candles, while all black, weren't black wax. They had been painted black."

"And?"

"It's obviously a poorly rendered copycat," Mary pointed out.

"Still don't see how that helps us. Erik—the one who supposedly made the first pentagram—is dead. Meaning, he wasn't on campus making the one that got burned down, and he hardly killed himself and moved his body."

"Obviously, but I wonder if his crime led to us having a more adept copycat." Kalinda jumped in.

"Great," I grumbled. Leaning back in my seat, I eyed both women before saying, "I know you all think I'm innocent. And I am. But how come you think it might be a copycat? I mean, shouldn't you be assuming it's my parents?"

"Your parents are dead."

"They are, although some say they faked their deaths. That it wasn't my mom they salvaged from the car. That my dad never died at all." I'd seen the rumors and even believed them for a tiny bit. Until time passed, and I remained alone, and realized they weren't coming back for me.

"If they were alive, do you really think your parents would jeopardize you?" asked Kalinda.

I hung my head. "No."

"Then we have a copycat. Possibly a friend of Erik's."

Or his killer.

22

I EMERGED FROM OUR MORNING HAIR-DYING session with a head of vivid pink locks and a whole lot of anxiety. We'd yet to hear anything.

The afternoon dragged. Kalinda roped me into helping her shop for groceries and then conscripted me into prepping for dinner. I had no idea what she was making, but it involved me fetching her ingredients and peeling more potatoes than I appreciated.

For entertainment, Mary put the crime scene photos on a loop on her laptop. Lucky me. I got to see it from every angle, including the body.

For a bully, Erik didn't look so tough in death. He didn't look scared, either. He didn't die with a smile on his face, but he didn't bear a screaming rictus either. He'd bled to death. The report had listed several wounds on his body but not a single ligature mark to show that he'd been bound. The logical assumption was that he'd been drugged, but police were awaiting a toxicology report to confirm, which would likely take a few days.

I studied those pictures of dead Erik more than I should have. Wondered if the MO was the same as the supposed pentagram murders in my old hometown. While I'd long proclaimed my parents' innocence, I did have questions about the case—even as my curiosity felt disloyal. How could I even think of blaming my parents? But then again, how could I remain willingly blind to the truth? I hadn't needed that mockumentary to point out the many coincidences.

If my parents hadn't committed any crimes, then they could surely have provided alibis for some of the murders. I could have vouched for them...only I would have been asleep when most of the incidents happened. People could sneak in and out with ease, as I well knew, which was why Joseph's insistence on shielding me was surprising.

How could he be so sure I'd not killed Erik? What about the new pentagram and its body? I'd supposedly been abed when the security guard had stumbled upon it. The cops had taken Joseph's word that his security system provided an alibi, yet knowing Mary, how easy would it be to change the logs?

Which led to me wondering if the professor might have an ulterior motive for providing me with a cover.

Could he be the killer? If yes, then it made no sense for him to send Jag to check out the body. Actually, sending Jag at all made no sense. He wasn't a forensic specialist.

Unless...

What if his sole purpose in seeing the body had to do with ridding it of evidence? Of all the possibilities, that fit the best. But it was just a theory. Could even be my paranoia talking. Why would people who'd gone out of their way to help me, betray me?

With that kind of turmoil inside my mind, I'd passed the stir-crazy point by late afternoon. Supper and dessert were in the oven. I'd helped with cleanup, and I had nothing left to do. Idle hands led to itchy feet.

"Want to go for a ride and grab some of our stuff?" Kalinda asked. "I need clothes and toiletries if I'm going to stay overnight."

"You're staying?" It should have occurred to me, given how completely she'd taken over the kitchen.

"Yes. I've already spoken to the professor about it. Even though you're posing as his niece, for propriety's sake, it would be best if another woman or two were around." She winked.

"Okay." It made sense. If someone hinted at impropriety, he could be ruined. "Anyone else staying?"

"Expect to see all of us coming and going."

"Won't that be weird, you guys all hanging at his place?"

"We'll handle it." A breezy reply as she swept out the door and dragged me in her wake.

Her driving involved a few life-threatening moments—not just for us but also for pedestrians—some musical yelling, and her beating her fastest time by a minute.

As we neared the place I'd recently called home, I noticed people on the sidewalk, pointing at the words spray painted across the red brick façade. Large, dripping, white block letters: *Killer*.

One guess as to who they meant.

This wouldn't end well.

I hunched down in the seat. "We should turn around and go back to the professor's house."

Kalinda kept going. "We need our things. What's the worst they can do? They're not about to assault two women in broad daylight."

I pursed my lips. "Don't be so sure about that."

She glanced at me. "You might have a point. It doesn't take much to set off a mob. We'll drive straight into the garage and enter the house via the kitchen."

"What if they block the driveway?" The pessimist in me saw how this could go wrong.

"Then I'll run them over."

"Kalinda!"

"Just kidding," she sang. But I wasn't entirely sure of that.

She kept her pace steady, and no one paid her any mind.

"I am going on the record as saying this is a bad idea." I sank as far down in my seat as I could.

Kalinda, being a little nuts, hit the gas, then slammed the brakes, spun the damned SUV on a dime, and turned into the driveway. Fearing for my life, I had to sit up and grab the oh-fucking-shit bar. She'd done a dangerous and yet skillfully sweet maneuver, acting so fast that only now did the people on the sidewalk start pointing and shifting. Before they could reach us, the car was in the garage, and the door—not ever fully open to start with— began to close.

"Ta-da!" she exclaimed. "Safe and sound."

"Except for the fact that I need to change my underwear," I grumbled as I got out of the car.

Too soon, as it turned out. I caught someone

peering under the door, yelling, "She's here! Slaughter Daughter is inside."

Well, shit. That wasn't good. I hugged myself. Leaving the professor's house seemed dumb now. I'd been safe there. Why had I let Kalinda talk me into coming? She didn't need me. Without me, she would have brazenly walked in the front door and demolished anyone who tried to block her path.

I wanted to be like her when I grew up. I chewed my lip and wished I'd stuck to those lessons on self-defense.

"Ignore them." Kalinda tugged me by the arm as she swept around the car, heading for the door inside. "You've done nothing. They're just trolls. Let's get our things." She moved with confidence into the house, but my steps were slower. I already had the things I needed most on me or at the professor's place.

Rather than grab the rest, I found myself gravitating to the living room, keeping out of sight of the windows. The crowd on the sidewalk grew and now included a few faces I recognized, like that girl from Professor Santino's social media class. So much for not perpetuating gossip. Maybe I'd report her to the professor and have her kicked out. Petty, but then again, so was her joining the mob to harass me. Their voices rose in a wordless clamor. The agitation humming through them penetrated the safety of the house, and I shivered.

Instinct told me to flee. And quickly.

"I think we should hurry," I yelled up the stairs.

"Almost done. Don't worry about the people outside. The doors are locked. We're fine."

As if to mock her words, a window broke, the shards hitting the floor in a noisy tinkle. I backed away as the culprit, a rock from the edge of the garden, rolled across the floor.

It only took one person to start violence.

Kalinda came flying out of her room and down the stairs, livid. "Those miscreants! How dare they?" She marched to the front door and flung it open to yell at the crowd. "Whoever broke the window, expect a visit from the cops, and a bill to replace it."

"We don't want a killer in our neighborhood!" was the bellowed reply.

"Abby isn't a killer, you Neanderthal." Kalinda's retort didn't help the situation.

A different person hollered, "Did you help her kill that kid?"

First off, Erik wasn't exactly a kid. Second, I knew she'd get caught up in my situation. "Close the door."

When someone yelled a rude slur, Kalinda

finally slammed the door and locked it. She turned a worried look my way. "They're quite unreasonable."

"I know." Left unsaid? *Welcome to my life.*

"I have enough things for now." She hefted a bag. "We should leave before they multiply."

With one window broken, it was only a matter of time before they swarmed the house.

"Not going to hear me argue."

We piled back into the Jeep, and she started it. She put her hand on the button to open the door, only to pause as we heard the thumping of fists hitting it. I glanced over my shoulder and saw the metal denting in multiple spots.

"I don't think you should open it."

"They wouldn't dare harm us." She didn't sound as sure as before.

"I think they *will* dare," I remarked. "This is my fault." I slid out of the vehicle, but before I could close the door, Kalinda leaned over.

"Where are you going?"

"They want me, not you. Maybe if I slip out the back, they'll let you go." Said even as I didn't believe it. As I'd feared, I'd dragged her into my mess and now didn't know how to get us out.

"What if they catch you!?" she hotly exclaimed.

"Better me than you." I offered a lopsided smile and closed the passenger-side door. I ignored the fists pummeling the metal shield that would soon buckle if they didn't stop. I headed for the house. Already in the kitchen, the back door was only a few paces away in the laundry-slash-mud room. I'd taken two steps when I froze at a sound from the hall.

Someone was inside.

Should I wait to see if they were friendly?

Like hell.

I headed for the laundry room and the door leading into the cemented-over rear yard. The fence around it stood about six feet. Climbing it would allow me to get to the other side of the block.

What I didn't count on was the fact that climbing meant yanking my body up and over. It took some huffing and heaving before I had one leg hiked over, holding on for dear life, just as a voice said, "What the fuck are you doing now?"

23

Falling, apparently.

Startled, I lost my grip, only I didn't hit the ground. Arms rescued me, and I looked into a familiar face. Mathews, whose first name I still didn't know.

"Hi," I said as he set me on my feet. "Thanks for catching me."

"Why are you climbing the fence?"

"There's a mob out front."

"Was a mob. The police just arrived and broke it up."

"So Kalinda's okay?"

"Kalinda is taking pictures of the damage and talking about suing loud enough for anyone lingering to hear."

"How did you get in the yard?"

He pointed behind. "Side gate was unlocked."

"And you just sauntered in."

"Yup. Figured you'd either stayed inside or decided to bolt."

"I'm not a fan of being torn limb from limb."

Rather than laugh and say I was exaggerating, he remained serious. "At least you were thinking. Now that the crowd's gone, you might want to think about going out the front door."

"I think someone was inside."

"That explains the piss-poor attempt at climbing."

"I would have been fine if you'd not startled me," I grumbled. Worst case, I fell and broke my neck. Hmm. Probably a good thing he interrupted.

"You're a veritable mountain goat, but my jeans are tight, and I'm not following."

"Who says I want you to follow?"

He rolled his eyes. "Do you really want to climb that fence?"

"Are you sure the mob is gone?"

"Most of them. A couple might have stayed behind because of the cops." He tugged me by the hand. "Come on. It's safe now."

Not entirely. I dug in my heels. "I don't want to deal with the cops."

"They're not here to arrest you."

"You don't know that for sure," I exclaimed.

"You can't hide in the yard forever. And you might want to move out of the house. It doesn't seem too safe."

"I've actually more or less moved out already. We were just grabbing some stuff."

"Then let me take you to your new home. Where are you staying?" He'd obviously not heard. Surprising, given campus rumors usually ran faster than the speed of light.

"I'd rather not go there yet. Do you have your car? Can we go for a ride?"

"Yeah. I'm parked the next block over."

I eyed the fence. "Give me a boost."

"I thought you weren't going to climb anymore."

"If I'm going to avoid people, then I can't go out the front. Give me a boost and pick me up on the other side."

He sighed. "Fine." I made it over intact with his help and moved quickly, lest the homeowner peek outside and see me using their yard as a shortcut.

I made it to the street before he did and took a minute to reply to Kalinda's text of: *Where are you??????*

I typed a short reply. *Safe.*

Where?

With a friend.

Was Mathews my friend? He did seem to have a habit of appearing when I needed someone.

Which, in retrospect, should have triggered my suspicion. His car rounded the block and slowed to let me in. Only as we sped away did I ask, "Why were you at the house?"

"I was hoping to talk to you."

"Really? What about?"

"Leaving town."

"Oh." Just a small, deflated sound.

He slammed the car to a stop and glanced at me. "Not for the reason you think. Fuck. Give me a second to find a place we can talk."

He ended up choosing a church parking lot of all places. An abandoned one showing crime scene tape fluttering across the door going inside. A shiver went through me.

"Isn't this where they found the first pentagram?" The fake one.

"Yeah. Sorry. I forgot about it." He grimaced, but when he would have thrown the car in reverse, I put my hand over his.

He stilled.

"It's okay. It's private, which is good, I guess. Unless you're planning to murder me." My laughter wasn't entirely false.

"I would never kill, but I will warn. I think you're in danger, Abby."

"Kind of late on that one, Mathews."

"Braedon. My name is Braedon."

"Nice to finally meet you," I teased.

His serious mien slipped into a half-smile. "I guess I never did properly introduce myself."

"Nope. Too busy giving me shit and now telling me to get out of your town."

"It's for your safety. Something's afoot, and you're in danger."

"Welcome to my life." I pushed out of his car and, with nowhere to go, headed for the church. The yellow tape fluttered against me as I passed.

I'd admit to a moment of trepidation when I entered the building, a little worried that I might get struck down. An atheist with suspected serial killer parents, I didn't believe in God. Yet at the same time, worried one existed.

The pews were wooden, once dark and gleaming, now dusty and scratched. Many had toppled and splintered, others held spray-painted messages that weren't very nice.

A crunch of debris from behind indicated that Braedon had followed.

I whirled. "Why do you keep coming to my rescue when it's clear you don't like me?"

"Never said I didn't like you. But I do think you should keep better company." He shoved his hands into his pockets, handsome and preppy. Solid, too, with a hint of a hard edge.

"Is this a warning about my friends?" I arched a brow.

"You can't trust them. They're not who you think," he insisted.

"Let me guess. I should trust you, though," I scoffed.

"I'm trying to help."

"By being bossy. And when questioned, intentionally vague."

"If I told you the truth, you wouldn't believe me."

I arched a brow. "How can you be so sure?"

"Because it took me seeing proof before I was convinced. And even then..." He rubbed a hand over his face. "You have to trust me when I say you're in danger. Your friends are lying to you."

"Says you."

"Why must you be so stubborn?"

"Why is that always the accusation when I won't unilaterally obey? I'm allowed to have an opinion, and, in the absence of proof, I form my own judgments. It tells me my friends aren't the problem."

He scrubbed a hand through his hair, tousling his blond locks. "There are things you don't know."

"Then tell me."

"I can't. I made a promise."

"Convenient," was my sarcastic reply.

"Not really. Because despite everything, in spite of my vow, I want to protect you." He sounded almost put out.

"I don't need saving."

"Are you sure about that?" A wryness imbued his query.

"Don't tell me your new mission in life is to save me from myself," I quipped.

"Do you think I want to feel this way? I think about you all the time."

"Creepy."

His eyes widened. Then he laughed. "I swear nothing nefarious."

"Big words."

"You're always sarcastic." He shook his head.

"It's a defense mechanism."

"You know, when I met you, knowing what I did, I expected someone different."

"Rough and tough bitch?" I asked.

"You're tough but soft, too. I'm pretty sure my last cat was more evil than you."

My lips twisted. "What an endorsement."

"You're special, Abby. I can't resist it even as I know I should."

"Try harder. Because you and I will never be a thing."

"Why not?"

I opened my mouth to say...what? It wasn't as if I had a boyfriend. Sure, Jag might have seduced me, but he'd made no promises. I remained unsure if he even liked me. "You're not my type." Too clean-cut. Too out of my league.

The very idea had me frowning. What made me think he was better than me?

"You haven't even given me a chance," he said, moving closer.

"It's not the right time."

He stared down at me. "Why?"

"Do I really need to spell it out? You've seen the shit happening around me."

"And? I know you're not a killer."

The statement had tears pricking the backs of my eyes. Why did I care what he thought? "My life's too complicated for a relationship."

"Even one that might ease the burden?"

"How?"

"By showing you're not alone," he said before he kissed me.

Where Jag had been all hard passion, Braedon was sweet sensuality. He kissed me as if we had all the time in the world, his mouth sweet and exploratory against mine, his hands firm on my waist.

His breath was hot. My blood surged. Awareness flared. Things might have gotten more heated, but my phone rang.

Since like only three people had my number, I couldn't exactly ignore it. Stepping away from Braedon and the passion boiling in my veins, I pulled out my cell just as the call went to voicemail. A text from Kalinda immediately followed.

You need to come home right now. They found another pentagram.

24

"I have to go."

"What's wrong?" Braedon grabbed my hands, but I couldn't meet his gaze. "Abby, tell me, what's got you so shaken."

He'd find out soon enough. "They found another pentagram."

"Where?"

I shrugged. "I don't know, but I'm guessing the cops want to talk to me about it because Kalinda says I need to go back to the professor's house asap."

"Professor?" His brow crinkled. "You're staying with a faculty member?"

"Yes. Apparently, Professor Santino is my uncle," I blurted. Seemed it didn't sound convincing, because Braedon's reply was sour.

"Since when?"

"Since my grandfather screwed around on my grandmother," I snapped. Yeah, I perpetuated the lie, but I didn't appreciate his attitude.

"When did you find out?"

"A few days ago," I mumbled.

"So you didn't know before moving here?" His brows rose. "And you both just happened to be here at the same time?"

The mother of all coincidences showed the weakness in the plan. I knew this charade wouldn't work, but it was all I had. "It's a small world, I guess."

"Pretty fucking small," Braedon muttered as we walked back to his car.

It occurred to me I'd never gotten to see the crime scene with its pentagram. Knowing another pentagram had been found, I'd lost my curiosity to see it.

Braedon didn't say much as he drove me to the professor's house. Angry. Simmering. And for what?

My tone conveyed my rancor. "For a guy who professes to like me, you can be a jerk. First, you condemned me based on who my parents were. Now, you're giving me attitude because of my uncle. Both things I have no control over, and I'm tired of being judged because of them."

He clenched the steering wheel. "I'm not mad

about that. More like pissed at the fact that you're being used."

"Used to do what?" I poked a hole in his theory. "Joseph lost his job because of me. The house I was staying in was vandalized. Teachers have asked me to drop their classes. And you're going to tell me the only people sticking by my side, the only ones who don't give a shit about my past, are the enemy?"

"Yes."

"Why? And don't tell me you can't explain."

His jaw tensed. "I don't have time now. Meet me later."

"Assuming I'm not arrested for something I didn't do." We pulled into the massive driveway. A police car was parked out front, and my favorite officer, Jenkins, stood on the front step. Even came to greet me as I stepped out of the passenger seat.

"Hello, officer."

"Where have you been?" Jenkins snapped, hand on his gun. Made me wonder if he slept with it. Probably.

"I was hanging with my friend." I gestured to Braedon. "Why?"

Rather than reply to that question, Jenkins smirked. "Does your boyfriend know you're cheating on him?"

First off, Jag was not my boyfriend. And, second,

would he be pissed? I both wanted him to be jealous and didn't.

"I should be going," Braedon declared. "Call me later."

He drove off, leaving me with Jenkins and his sneer. "Planning a hookup?"

"Yes, as a matter of fact. Braedon's going to help me work on being an asshole in case I decide to follow in your career footsteps." I could have been nice. Polite. But Jenkins annoyed the fuck out of me.

I entered the house to find half of the gang there. The professor stood by the fireplace, Kalinda served cookies and coffee, while Cashien sat on the couch beside Mary, who of course, held an open laptop. I didn't see Peter, Jackson, or Jag and wondered if they were in the house or still out.

How had Jag's visit with the body gone?

"Abby." My fake uncle beamed. "I trust your outing was enjoyable."

Not really, but I lied. "Yes, it was. I assume there's a reason our friendly local PD is visiting?"

"We found another pentagram," Walters declared.

"And rushed over to accuse me. You shouldn't have." They ignored my sarcasm as I flopped onto the couch.

Walters had his notebook out. "You recently

lived here, correct?" He showed me the address of the house I shared with Kalinda and the others.

"Yes."

"During our investigation of a crime at that location—"

"A crime you've yet to arrest anyone for," Kalinda huffed.

"Ma'am, vandalism pales in comparison to what they found in that basement."

"A basement you didn't have a warrant to search," Cashien interjected.

"We were securing the premises when a penta-gram was discovered," Walters declared. "The fluid found at the scene has been sent for processing. Investigators are currently gathering evidence."

I rolled my eyes. "And, of course, you think I created it."

"Doubtful, given my niece has been staying with me," the professor smoothly lied.

Walters' mustache wiggled. "The blood was fresh. And, apparently, she was inside the house today."

"I didn't do it." The only defense I had. But it wouldn't matter if someone planted hair or some-thing of mine with it.

Jenkins was the one to glance at his phone as it beeped and then leaned down to whisper in Walters' ear loud enough that we could all hear. My blood ran cold at what he said.

When Walters turned his gaze on me, I could see him bubbling with triumph. "They've matched the blood at the crime scene in the basement to Mr. Jerome."

Oh. Shit.

"I don't know how it got there. It wasn't me." I could feel the trap springing shut on me.

Jenkins grinned in glee as he hitched his pants and said, "We are going to have to continue downtown."

"Am I being arrested?"

The professor stepped in. "You do realize Abby is not the only person living in that house, right?"

Kalinda hurried to add, "And the basement is always locked. None of us ever went down there, and only the landlord has the key."

I could have added more to that, such as the fact that I didn't even know we had a basement. Not that I would have checked it out. Basements were creepy.

"Given her past, I'm afraid we need to question her further." Walters almost sounded apologetic.

Again, I didn't have to defend myself as my new friends stepped up, with Cashien interjecting, "Not without a lawyer present. No one questions her without me." Was he allowed to be my legal counsel? Had he passed the bar?

"We'll wait for you, but she rides with us." Walters stood and tucked his notebook away. Jenkins pulled out a zip strip.

The professor protested. "There's no need to tie her hands. She's no danger to anyone."

"We've got a dead kid she had a grudge against." Jenkins' eyes gleamed, the excitement in them barely contained.

I just felt sick and tired. I held out my wrists. The truth didn't matter. My innocence, either. "I'll go. I have nothing to hide." I tried not to wince as the plastic bit into my flesh when Jenkins tightened it more than necessary.

"Let's go." Jenkins tugged me, and I ducked my head, hiding the tears brimming in my eyes.

I barely heard the rush of promises— "Don't worry, we'll have you out before bedtime." "Stay calm." "I'll keep dinner warm."—as we headed out the door. Only to almost slam into Walters, who froze on the front step, phone to his ear.

"Say that again," Walters snapped. Then, after a pause, "You do know I have her in custody?"

I held my breath, realizing he was speaking about me.

"Are you sure?" Walter asked. Then sighed.

"Yeah. I hear you." Walters hung up and turned to Jenkins. "Cut her loose."

"What?"

"Let her go. Captain's orders."

"You've got to be kidding. She's a killer." Jenkins sounded genuinely baffled.

"Not according to the person who turned themselves in and is claiming they did it."

My turn to exclaim, "What? Who confessed?"

Walters ignored me. "Gotta cut her loose."

"I don't have scissors." Said by the disappointed cop.

"I'll get some." Kalinda, who'd followed, went running back inside.

Without waiting to see if I'd been set free or even offering an apology, Walters and Jenkins got into their car and left. It wasn't until my hands were cut loose that we found out who they'd arrested.

Jag.

25

THE PROFESSOR AND CASHIEN WOULDN'T LET ME join them at the police station. Which meant I got to pace as Kalinda cooked, and Mary hacked.

As for Peter and Jackson...who knew? Of my roommates, I knew them the least.

I went to bed before anyone came home, dropping into a restless sleep where I dreamed that someone chased me. And then I was doing the chasing. Only to be caught!

I thrashed and woke to find myself in someone's arms, a deep voice growling, "Stop fighting me."

"Jag?" I said. Then added more urgently, "Are you okay?"

"Yeah." He snuggled in beside me, and I smelled fresh shampoo as if he'd recently showered.

Which begged the question. "Why are you in my bed?"

"Keeping an eye on you," he grumbled as he snaked an arm around me and cradled me against his body.

"I'm in bed. Can't exactly get into trouble." Tell that to my racing heart. It wanted to get into all kinds of trouble.

"Tired. Long night," he mumbled against me.

I might have argued more but for the gentle snore and the fact that I rather enjoyed the way he held me. Cuddling wasn't something I indulged in often. Most of my relationships proved short-lived.

I spent my first night in a guy's arms and woke to him nuzzling my hair—a definite boner pressing against my ass.

Or was it a morning pee? Because I sure as heck had to go.

"Hey," he mumbled.

"Hey." And then because I lacked a romantic bone in my body, I said, "I've got to go to the bathroom. I'll be right back." A horrifying thought hit as I shut the door behind me.

Did he think I was doing a number two? What if I farted while I peed and he heard? Or came in after and smelled it?

When he'd crawled into bed with me last night,

I'd been half-asleep, shocked and intrigued by having Jag in my bed. Now, he was actually there. Possibly with a hard-on.

For me.

And here I was, wasting time in the bathroom. Not only men thought with their crotches.

I peed, then as I washed my hands, I gave my girl parts a quick scrub. Brushed my teeth. Washed my face. Untangled my hair. Stared in the mirror at my wide eyes staring back.

What was happening here? I had Jag in my bed. But what about Braedon? I'd kissed him the day before. But, technically, I'd kissed Jag first.

I glanced at the closed door. I really wanted to kiss Jag again, and it wasn't as if Braedon had asked me to be his girlfriend or anything. Nor had Jag. Yet he'd crawled into my bed last night. When he was tired and looking for a safe spot to crash, he chose me of all people.

I emerged after taking a deep breath of courage.

He was waiting for me, a slow smile curving his lips. "Took you long enough."

My cheeks flamed. Dammit, now he really thought I'd pooped. So romantic.

He held up the comforter, showing off that he wore track pants and nothing else. No one could resist a bare-chested Jag this early in the morning.

Hell, yeah, I crawled in beside him, getting a cheap thrill as his arm came around me, tugging me close, cocooning me against his body. Despite being warm, I shivered.

"Cold?" he asked, the breath of the word a sigh across my skin.

On the contrary, heat spread through me. "Not anymore."

The hand on my belly began to move, rubbing across fabric. Then the fingers tugged at the hem of my shirt and paused as if asking for permission.

I squirmed against him, pushing my ass against his erection, clear despite his pants. It kind of stole my breath, which hitched as Jag's fingers crept under the fabric, teasing my flesh.

I shivered again and sighed. He touched me, his hands skimming up under fabric to cup my breasts and play with the nipples.

The sensation had me gyrating, my hips rolling and moving as I sought to ease the building ache between my thighs. Feeling bold, I grabbed his hand and slid it down to cup my mound.

In that moment, despite not truly understanding how I felt about him, I wanted the release he offered —the pleasure.

I'd not had sex often. Not because I didn't crave it, but for other more complicated reasons. I always had to hide myself because most people couldn't see past my family origins. But Jag knew, and Jag didn't appear to care.

And I was too aroused to wonder about his motives. I just wanted to feel.

I turned so I could face him.

His fingers lightly traced the edge of my face, and he stared at me with an expression I'd call fond, if a bit confused—but definitely smoldering with arousal.

That, I could handle.

I kissed him.

He groaned. He also rolled me onto my back. My arms went around his neck to hold him close as I pressed my lips to his. The heat between us erupted.

So much heat. As we kissed, I touched him, finally able to run my hands over his taut flesh. I dug my nails in when he wedged his thigh between mine and applied pressure. I rode his leg for a few grinds before he groaned. Then his hands stripped me of my pajamas, which consisted of loose shorts, a T-shirt, and prim and proper panties.

No one liked to be naked alone. I tugged at his track pants until he was just as bare as I was.

Jesus, no wonder I could feel him through his pants. His size had me clenching. I may have even had a mini-orgasm.

We came together in a clash of flesh that sizzled. There was something decadent about how we fit together. How good it all felt.

Nothing was said. A good thing because it would have probably reminded me of the insanity of my actions. Was now the time to be screwing around?

As he fingered my clit, rubbing until I panted, I only knew I wanted this. Him. Inside me. Making me come.

I reached for him, growling as he kept himself just out of reach. "Come here."

"Are you sure?"

I couldn't believe he asked. I dragged him down for a heated kiss. His head pressed against me. My thighs parted wide to accommodate him. His mouth caught my cry of pleasure as he sank into me, taking his sweet time, making me feel every stretching inch. As he pushed into me, I dug my nails into his shoulders.

He fucking paused again. "You okay?" he whispered into my mouth.

My legs wrapped around him in reply. He groaned, and his forehead pressed against mine as he began a slow, torturous rhythm, digging deep with his cock until I writhed under him, moaning aloud. He quickened his pace, the deeper strokes stealing my voice, I could only hold on and ride the wave that crested. I shuddered. I orgasmed, my body rigid and then undulating in pleasure.

He kept hitting that spot.

Kept smacking into my sweet fucking spot. I bit him as I came even harder the second time. He uttered a grunt and a growl, then froze, buried deep inside me, his cock pulsing as he came. He didn't crush me when he finally relaxed, but he did keep his forehead leaned against mine as our breathing normalized.

I opened my eyes to find him staring at me.

Had he been watching me the entire time? I'd had my eyes closed as I rode the pleasure.

As our gazes locked, I said, "Good morning."

I could feel his smile as he rumbled, "Yes, it is." He shifted, and I trembled.

Shyness hit me. I didn't know what to say now. What if I spoke the wrong words and ruined...whatever this was?

Suddenly, his head jerked to the side as if he'd heard something. His expression took on that of a hunter, intent and focused.

"What's wrong?" I whispered. Was someone in the hall? Had they heard us? I'd die of embarrassment.

Jag leaned down to brush his mouth against mine

and whispered, "If they ask, I was here with you all night."

Before I could say a word, I heard commotion in the hall a second before someone flung open my bedroom door.

Jag rolled off me, but it was too late to hide. The professor swept in, wearing a scowl, and he wasn't alone.

26

NOTHING LIKE GETTING CAUGHT NAKED IN BED
with my lover, his cum leaking from me, to wish I'd
skipped the whole college thing and gone straight to
work. Sure, it would have been a low-paying gig that
might not have gotten me far in life, but it beat the
embarrassment of having an audience.

The professor huffed. "I told you they were both
here. And have been all night, as you can see."

Jag pushed up to a sitting position. "What the
fuck? Ever hear of knocking?"

I sank under the blankets, too hot-cheeked to
face anyone.

Walters barked, "Don't get mouthy with me.
How long have you been here?"

"Me? Since last night. And in case it's not clear, I
wasn't sleeping alone," drawled Jag.

Definitely dying, especially since I heard Jenkins muttering, "It's a wonder she's got time to get in trouble given how much she gets around."

I felt Jag stiffen beside me. He didn't know about Braedon. Would he care if he knew we'd kissed?

"Watch your mouth," interjected my fake uncle.

"We need to question them."

"Then you can do so once they've gotten dressed. Or would you like to explain this abuse of power?" The professor never got mad—he just got smart.

"Get dressed and meet us downstairs. We have some questions."

To which Jenkins added, "Don't try to leave, or we'll track you down and drag you in."

Walters coughed.

Jenkins grumbled, "Not literally, of course, but you will answer."

"To what?" I asked.

The professor eyed me as he said, "We'll speak about it when you're ready. Officers?" He swept a hand that forced them to leave the room.

The door slammed shut, and I groaned into the mattress. "Fuck."

Being a guy, Jag chuckled. "We did."

Angling my head, I eyed him suspiciously. "How

did you know they were coming here?" Was that why he'd seduced me?

"I didn't. But this does work out well. At least now, they'll stop acting as if we're faking our relationship."

Wait, did this put us in a relationship? Aloud I said, "They thought we were lying?"

"They are supposed to detect that kind of thing." His lip lifted at the corner.

"But we're not...That is..." I stammered. "What exactly are we?"

"About to be questioned." He rolled off the bed, giving me a view of his ass. Nice. I could have sunk my teeth into it.

However, with the cold bucket of cops waiting downstairs, rational thought resumed. I couldn't help but wonder why Jag had come to my bed. Had he known to expect the police?

He headed for the bathroom, and I didn't care if he'd touched and seen every inch of my naked body as we fucked. My modest ass went for my knapsack of clothes. I managed a bra and shirt before he emerged. Head ducked because I couldn't look him in the eye for some reason, I took my panties and slacks into the bathroom with me.

No condom during our little rendezvous meant jizz rolling down my leg. I was on the pill, so I didn't worry about getting pregnant, but dumb-dumb me, apparently, I wanted to catch a disease.

There really needed to be a better way to ask a guy in the heat of the moment when he'd gotten tested last. Always awkward. I'd not had sex in a while and had two clean blood workups since. I took that kind of thing seriously, having seen what it could do to the body in my biology classes. I should have asked him to put on a rubber. Usually would have. But Jag...there was just something about the guy.

I emerged to find him waiting for me. "Ready?" he asked, arching a dark brow.

I breathed out hard. "No."

He grabbed my hands and drew me close. The gesture startled me. I met his gaze.

"It will be okay."

"You can't know that. What do they want? I don't even know what happened to you at the police station. Why were you arrested?" We'd not had a chance to talk with our voices. But our bodies? Best conversation ever.

"Security caught me poking around at the morgue."

"And arrested you?"

"Yeah, charged me with trespassing. The prof

sprang me, and I was supposed to go home. But then I heard about the pentagram they found."

"And you confessed to it."

"Yeah. It's not a big deal."

"It is to me. I'm glad the professor got you out."

"Wasn't him, actually. Turns out they found footage of the person who made the pentagram that caught on fire."

Given the cops were here... My shoulders slumped. "They think it's me."

He shook his head. "No. The video exonerated us both."

"What *does* it show?"

"No idea. They wouldn't say. But, apparently, it was enough to let me go. The professor brought me here, and rather than find a cold bed, I chose yours." His lips quirked.

So it wasn't an accident. "What time did you join me, in case they ask?"

"Eleven, right after the prof and I grabbed some pizza. I was starving, so we brought a few boxes home."

Eleven? I'd still been awake. And I knew for a fact that I'd been sleeping for a bit before he crawled into bed with me. Meaning he lied.

He eyed me. Waiting.

"Still can't believe you woke me to ask if I wanted a slice." I built on our story.

His eyes danced with amusement. "Lucky me, your hunger was of another sort."

I blushed. He dragged me closer and kissed me. A kiss that told me not to worry. An embrace that held promise.

He let go of me and moved to the door, swinging it open. He held out his hand.

I slipped my fingers into his, and we went downstairs towards the sounds of voices coming from the living room where Mary, Kalinda, and the professor were gathered.

Walters and Jenkins weren't the only cops waiting for us. A woman in a dark suit, her hair in a multitude of tight braids, sat on a chair, holding a notepad. She looked over as we entered.

I noticed the tears on Kalinda's cheeks. The shock on Mary's face. My fingers tightened on Jag's, and he drew me into his body.

"Hello, again, Mr. Stallone." The policewoman's gaze turned on me. "You are Abby Smith?"

His last name was Stallone? I wanted to giggle and ask him if he knew Sylvester, but the serious lady stole all the mirth from the room.

I nodded but felt a need to add, "It's actually Abby Baker now."

The woman's lips pursed. "I'm Detective Wilson, Special Victims Unit."

"Why are you here?" Jag asked. "Last night at the station, I thought you had a video that cleared shit up."

"We are here on a different matter." Wilson then proceeded to knock the air out of me when she said, "Peter Morris was found dead in the wee hours of the morning under suspicious circumstances."

27

UNDER SUSPICIOUS CIRCUMSTANCES WAS ANOTHER term for murdered, and it hit close to home. I knew Peter. Not well, but enough for it to shock me. I spent that morning and the ensuing interview in a haze as Wilson hammered my friends and me with questions.

Yes, I'd been home all evening with a few people as witnesses. No, I'd not left. Yes, Jag came home before midnight. No, he didn't leave my bed—an admission that left my cheeks smoking hot. It didn't help that Jenkins smirked. Such an unpleasant fellow. Wilson while no-nonsense, at least didn't have any snide remarks to offer, and she kept the cop duo in line.

The professor showed the security system logs to

prove that the house had been locked up tight and hadn't opened until the cops knocked the next day.

"You don't mind if we have a forensic specialist go over these to check for tampering?" Wilson asked.

My fake uncle offered a wide smile as he said, "Be my guest. We have nothing to hide."

A complete and utter lie, but I wasn't about to blow it wide open. For some reason, the professor and the gang had chosen to circle the proverbial wagons around me to provide a ring of protection. It both elated and terrified because I'd yet to figure out why they were watching over me. Why did they care?

At one point, the detective asked, "Professor Santino, can you explain why it appears as if all these students are living with you? It seems ill-advised and unusual."

Unusual to me was the fact that the professor seemed acquainted with my roommates. Which, in retrospect, I should have questioned. Given they were supposedly new here, how did they all know each other so well? Obviously, I'd missed something important—the piece that would make some sense of this puzzle.

"It might seem unorthodox for the students to be living here, yet what else could I do when vandals intent on harassing my newly discovered niece rendered their house inhabitable? The place needs major repairs and isn't safe, leaving them homeless. It seemed only right to offer my niece's friends the use of my place, given it is large enough to accommodate."

The man could act. Holy shit. If I didn't know better, I'd have believed his seemingly emotional face as the professor spread his hands and delivered his speech. "And before you worry about me influencing some of their grades, I should mention that I've taken a leave of absence."

"Why?" Wilson's gaze sharpened.

"Because I am an author. Do you read?" He adeptly whipped a book out of nowhere, a man with a smoldering expression posed on the cover.

Wilson's eyes widened, and then she blushed. "I can't. Rules and all."

"Ah, yes. Mustn't look like you're accepting a bribe. No problem. Perhaps, instead, I shall donate many books to the precinct and the local library to thank you for the fine work you do."

"The library is a great idea."

I couldn't believe how the professor had Wilson eating out of his hand. It was elegantly done, and I could see Jenkins falling under his spell, as well—his posture easing, his hand nowhere near his gun.

The questions ended not long after, and with the

cops unable to ruin our alibis or trip up our stories, they left. But no one sighed in relief.

"Fuck!" Kalinda uttered quite eloquently, looking appropriately tragic with her wet cheeks, yet her posture poised and strong. She was the first to move. "This kind of news needs a mimosa."

"A jug. Easy on the juice." Cashien's suggestion.

"And a ton of bacon," Jag declared. "We're going to need protein to get through the day."

They spoke casually with a dark humor that appalled.

"Seriously?" I exclaimed. "You're going to eat and drink? Our friend is dead." More their friend than mine. How could they be so calm? Apart from Kalinda's tears, they didn't seem angry or all that sad.

"And you think we're not going to find out what happened?" The professor sounded chiding. "Mary?"

She held up her laptop. "I've got the report and skimmed it. Same MO as Erik. Drained of blood and dumped."

"Have they found another pentagram?" Jag asked.

Mary shook her head. "Not yet, at any rate. They're still waiting to identify the victim of the pentagram at the college. It looks the same as the others but was interrupted. With three bodies, they're now saying we've got a serial killer."

"How many until they call in the FBI?" I rubbed my forehead.

"Depends on how hard the precinct gets shamed in the media since it's contained to the campus," Jag drawled.

The media. Shit. Bad enough the people crowding my house had been aiming their phones at me. I'd inadvertently seen that I remained just as unphotogenic as before. "This is going to get ugly."

"Yes," the professor said as Kalinda whipped around the kitchen, getting the juice maker going, finding some champagne—because every kitchen kept a few bottles, as everyone knew.

The professor must really be doing well at the whole writing thing.

"Now would be a good time to drive me to a train station. You don't want me around now that the shit has hit the fan," I said.

The backlash would be astronomical. The internet was a cruel and vicious place. People were mean.

The good news was that it did eventually die down, though it never fully went away. Like a rash, it returned. You suffered, and then you waited for the cycle to start again.

Fuck me, I was tired of it. I put my head on the granite counter.

Kalinda slid a mimosa in front of me. "Drink."

"I don't want to drink. Or to eat. I want this to stop. I need this bullshit to go away," I exclaimed. Shoving away from the counter, I stormed from the kitchen in a full-blown tantrum, expecting them to come after me.

No one called me to return. Jag didn't follow.

That hurt, even though it shouldn't have.

We'd had sex. Not all sex meant a relationship. The logic didn't help. I remained pissed.

Stomping to my room, I slammed the door and then paced. Simmered. I lasted three minutes before I wondered what the fuck I was doing.

Would I really stick around as some asshole tried to frame me? Would I let the media storm about to descend not only sweep me into the churning viciousness but snag my friends, too?

I grabbed my knapsack and quickly stuffed it. It would be best for everyone if I left. People might live longer, too. After all, Peter had died. Erik was dead. And what about the third body in the pentagram? Want to bet the victim would somehow be linked to me, too? Hell, it might even be Jackson. When was the last time anyone saw him?

Fuck.

I needed out of this house. Had to get away from these people. What if Kalinda was next? And then there was the fact that they could so calmly eat and drink as one of their friends lay cold on a slab. Would any of them care if I left?

Jag...

He never even came to check on me. Never mind I'd stomped off only about seven minutes ago.

I snuck down the stairs, worried about every perceived creak. I saw and heard no one. The alarm system remained unarmed. I exited via the front door, expecting to hear someone yell at me to come back. I quickly moved down the driveway and into the road, walking briskly as I pulled out my phone and hesitated. Who could I call?

All my friends were back at the professor's house. Except for one.

Ten minutes later, and four weaving blocks away at a coffee shop, Braedon picked me up.

I heaved a sigh as I leaned against the headrest on the passenger side of his car. "Thanks."

"I heard what happened." No shit. I doubted anyone *hadn't*. "Were you close to Peter?"

"No. Not really. I mean, we were roommates, and I saw him around, but we never talked much."

"The cops are saying we might have a serial killer copycatting the pentagram killings."

My lips turned down. "I am aware, trust me. They keep trying to pin it on me. The problem being I've got alibis for their dates and times."

Braedon spoke carefully as he said, "Word on the street is they think Jag did it."

"If the cops thought he did it then why did they let him go?"

"Because he's got a supposedly airtight alibi." He glanced at me. Was that condemnation or pity in his gaze?

"Jag's not a killer." The man who'd snuggled me and made my body sing couldn't be a murderer.

"Are you sure?" Braedon's tone turned harsh. "Don't be so blind to the truth. Your friends aren't who you think they are. I've been looking into them, Abby."

"Why?"

He didn't reply at first, and I could see him stalling as if looking for the right words. The right lie.

"Why have you been spying on them?" I repeated.

"Surely, you can see it. Something's not right about them."

"Because they're Slaughter Daughter's friends?" I snapped.

"That has nothing to do with it. I know who you are, and I'm your friend—hoping to be something more." He put his hand on my leg, a light touch, and I burned with shame and guilt.

I had nothing to be ashamed of. Jag and I had exchanged no promises. And Braedon confused me.

"You hated me the first time we met," I reminded.

"Because I knew who you were. I recognized you. And I admit, I might have believed some of the media hype. Only you were a lot different than I expected."

"Different how?" Was I uglier? Stupid?

I was wrong on all counts.

"Attractive. The pics I saw didn't do you justice."

"I'm aware," I grumbled.

"Then I started talking to you and realized you were smart. And strong. Despite being attacked, you didn't back down. You've been doing your best to hold your head high in spite of everything."

His vision of me stroked my ego nicely. However, he ignored the ugliness. "It's great you see all those things, but other people don't. Once they realize I'm in their neighborhood, their city, I become a joke. A scapegoat for every ugly crime. They purposely get in my face to get a reaction. Or they whisper about me as I go by. They'll take videos and pics, post them

EVE LANGLAIS

online with the dumbest captions. And anyone with me will become part of the sick game."

"That's brutal."

"It's my life." And I'd learned to handle it. Crying achieved nothing. Standing and facing the condemnation meant listening to daily abuse. Leaving, though... It solved all my problems.

"I'm sorry I was one of those assholes who judged you without knowing you first."

"Apology accepted. Now how about doing the same for my friends?"

"Your friends are liars."

"What have they lied about?" I asked.

"Did you know they're not actually registered for college?"

"What are you talking about? Of course, they're students."

Braedon shook his head. "Actually, they're not."

"But they told me... Why would they lie?"

"To get close to you."

"To do what? Get in trouble? Because so far, knowing me hasn't exactly helped them out," I snapped.

He shrugged. "I don't know their plan, but it can't be good. Not given what they are. Pure evil."

I blinked. My lying roommates might be many

things. But evil? "I assure you, they're not demon spawn."

"You're wrong about that. They are actually demons."

28

OTHER THAN LAUGHTER, I DIDN'T THINK A REPLY to that kind of statement existed. I howled until I almost cried.

Braedon seethed. A good look for the blond surfer boy. "It's true."

I controlled my giggles enough to say, "Are you on drugs?"

"I know it sounds crazy—"

"Very," I interrupted. "Which is why you're going to stop this car so I can get out."

Only he didn't slow down. "You have to believe me. Jag and the others, they're demons."

"And how do you know this? Because I can assure you, Jag doesn't have a tail." To think I'd entertained an interest in Braedon. Good thing I'd discovered his crazy side before things went anywhere.

"I know because someone opened my eyes to the truth. Your friends, and possibly that professor, are demons."

"They look pretty human," I drawled.

"Because they enchant their true shape so that they can blend in."

The laughter bubbled again. "Holy shit. You're just doubling down on the insanity."

"I can prove it."

"Go ahead."

"I have to contact her. She can show you the proof."

"She?"

"Selena. I don't know her last name," he admitted. "She contacted me after seeing us together and told me I should get you away from the spawn before they hurt you."

"Do you believe every crazy chick who tells you stories about supposed demons?" I arched a brow. Probably not a good idea to antagonize him, but the weird thing about this was how reasonable he sounded. As if this were fucking normal.

It wasn't. More than ever, I regretted not telling anyone where I'd gone.

"Selena showed me the truth, Abby. Showed me how they hide among us, pretending they're human.

But they're not. They're killers." Braedon spoke with conviction.

I shook my head. "You're wrong."

"You have to believe me, Abby. You're in great danger." The sincerity deserved an academy award.

My phone went off. I ignored it.

Braedon pulled over near a strip mall. It made me feel marginally better to have people around. "Give me a chance to show you. To prove what I'm saying."

"If this Selena saw me with demons, then why tell you? Why not approach me?"

"She's afraid she'll tip them off if she comes near you. Do you even realize how much they keep you under observation?"

If they were students, running into them often on campus was normal. If they weren't students, though...

My phone pinged again. Another text message followed by ringing. I kept it tucked in my lap as if it weren't the most annoying thing in the world at the moment. "Can you drive me to a bus or train station?"

"You want to leave?"

"Can you blame me?" was my bitter reply.

"But the police... The investigation."

"Right now, I've lucked out on alibis. What if I don't have one to shield me from the next murder?"

Braedon reached for my hand, and I let him hold it. "You don't have to run, Abby. I can protect you. I'll find a way to expose the real monsters."

"You're going to prove demons exist?" I snorted.

"I will do whatever it takes to protect you." He dragged me close and kissed me, not the soft embrace of before but a passionate thing that left me feeling hot and guilty.

Jag and I might not have truly talked about anything, but kissing another guy felt wrong.

As I pulled away, a motorcycle pulled up alongside us.

A second later, Jag yanked Braedon from the car.

29

OH, SHIT. JAG WAS GOING TO PUNCH BRAEDON. IT was hot. Wrong.

Still fucking hot.

I scrambled out of the car. "Don't hit him!"

Jag's fist stilled, and Braedon smirked as he stood unafraid. "Go ahead and hit me. I'm sure the video evidence from the plaza security will be enough, with my complaint, to put your ass in jail where it belongs."

"What are you doing with Abby?" Jag growled. Alpha male pissing to mark his territory.

Again, way sexier than it should be. I'd never had a guy jealous over me before.

"What does it look like I was doing?" Braedon deliberately taunted, and my shame burned bright, then flipped to guilt as Jag shot me a glance that held anger and pain.

"Let go of Braedon."

"Why are you with him?" Jag replied instead.

"I called him for a ride."

"If you needed a lift, you should have asked me." Shoving Braedon away from him, Jag whirled to face me fully.

I shrugged. "Didn't figure you'd take me to the bus station, what with you stuffing your face to mourn the loss of your friend." It wasn't a fair accusation.

Jag snarled. "What else am I supposed to do? Run away? How's that working for you so far?"

It hit me like a slap. My lips pursed. Braedon's smirk reminded me of what he'd said. "Are you enrolled with the college?"

"What?"

"You heard me. Are you and the others actually students?"

Jag opened and closed his mouth.

Answer enough. "Unbelievable," I muttered. "What was I? Some kind of sick game for you and your friends?"

"It's not like that."

"Not like what? You lied to me," I yelled. "All of you."

EVE LANGLAIS

"I can explain."

"No." I waved a hand. "I don't care. I'm done with you. Him. This town. Everything."

I began to walk and was flanked by both guys, arguing at me and over me.

"Come on, buttercup, you can't leave."

"Abby can do whatever she likes," Braedon countered. "You heard her. Leave her alone."

"If you don't shut your mouth, I'm going to ruin the thousands your parents spent on orthodontics," Jag yelled, losing his cool.

I really believed he would. Which was why I turned to Braedon and said, "It's time you left."

At my firm expression, he sagged, only to add, "Are you sending him away, too?"

"I will, after Jag and I have a chat."

"About?"

I thinned my lips. "None of your fucking business."

Braedon didn't look happy, and his stride was stiff as he stalked off. I felt shitty. He'd not done anything bad to me. My anger was mostly over *my* stupidity. I'd known I should stay away from Jag. Instead, I'd slept with him.

The moment we were alone, Jag just had to double-down. "What a prick."

"Is he? He's not the one lying to me."

"Don't kid yourself. He's just trying to get in your pants."

He deserved the slap I delivered. Jag's head barely turned, and he worked his jaw as he drawled, "Feel better?"

"No! Why did you and the others lie about being students? Was it to spy on me?"

"Yes."

He didn't deny it, and I blinked. "Why? Worried I'm a killer like my parents?"

"Nope."

"Then why, dammit?" I was getting so tired of the non-answers.

"It's complicated."

I slapped him again and could admit to enjoying it a bit more than I should.

This time, he licked his lower lip and winked at me. "Maybe there is more of a killer inside you than expected."

I should have been appalled at my violence. Instead, I lifted my chin. "Going to hit me back?"

He chuckled. "The only hitting I'm doing with you will be the kind we did in bed. Where you claw my back and demand more."

From pissed to blushing. The desire to climb him like a tree hit. And he saw it. Damn him.

He reached for me, and I almost gave in to it.

Almost melted into his lying arms just so I could taste those false lips.

I shook my head and stepped away. "No. I'm not falling for that again."

"Buttercup." He purred my name.

"You lied to me. All of you."

"We had our reasons. Tell you what, come back to the house with me, and we'll tell you everything."

"Bullshit. You're just saying that so I'll go with you. Tell me here. Now."

"I can't. It's—"

"Don't say complicated. According to Braedon, you want to kill me because you're demons."

"Do I look like a demon?" He reached for me, and I didn't move in time. He dragged me close, and I didn't fight despite my reluctance. He still felt good. "Does this feel demonic to you?" His mouth pressed to mine, his lips demanding, hard.

I melted. I was weak. Hungry. Needy.

He fed me his passion, and I craved more. His hands on my ass, grinding me into him, weren't enough. I remembered how he'd felt inside me.

He whispered into my mouth, "Come home with me, and I'll show you how much I want you."

Maybe I should. He'd come after me. He did seem to care.

Wait. I pushed away from him. "How did you find me?"

"I followed you."

I arched a brow. "And while on your motorcycle, you couldn't catch up to me the four blocks I walked to the corner store?"

"I followed you a different way once I realized you were gone."

My eyes widened. "Did you plant a tracker on me?"

"We kind of had to, given the shit that's been happening."

"Had to? Fuck off. I never gave you permission."

"It's for your own safety, buttercup."

"No, it's part of the game you're playing. You and your friends. Except, I'm out. Done with this bullshit." I threw up my hands before walking away.

30

THE ASSHOLE HADN'T COME AFTER ME.

What kind of a dumb bitch was I that I was pissed he hadn't?

I made it all the way to the bus station on foot, only to find that all seats were sold out. I bought a ticket for the next day and then rented a motel room.

I didn't plan to leave that space until it was time for my departure. I couldn't help but have questions. So many. I didn't believe Braedon's story about my friends being demons, but I couldn't help but wonder the others' end game. What purpose did befriending me serve?

Unless... Were they dabbling in murder and planning to use me as a scapegoat? Only, why kill Peter? Wasn't he part of their group?

Around eight p.m., I went for ice and to hit a

vending machine—safer than any store. I'd been followed around before while shopping. The running commentary on my choice of junk food ruined my love of snack cakes. Vending machines tended not to shame me for my choices.

A scan of the parking lot showed few cars and fewer rooms with lights on. As my gaze tracked back, I glanced across the street and saw a vehicle I recognized. I marched over and knocked on the window.

A figure slouched in the front rose as the glass descended. Mary grinned sheepishly at me. "Hey, Abby."

"Why are you spying on me?"

"Just making sure you're safe."

"From what?"

"Bad things." A weak reply, along with her half-hearted shrug.

"Unfucking believable," I snapped. "Would it kill someone to give me a straight answer?"

"It's complicated."

"Tell you what; you can be complicated without me. I'm leaving town."

"You can't."

"Can't?" I arched a brow. "Give me a single good reason to stay."

"Because we can fix this. Fix it so it never happens again."

"You're too late to fix anything. I'm Slaughter Daughter, and that will never change." And times like these, I wondered if I should live up to the title. I wondered what my next shrink would say when I claimed judgmental people turned me into a homicidal maniac. After all, tell someone something enough times, and they start to believe it.

"We can help you," Mary insisted. "Have been helping you for longer than you realize."

"I call bullshit on that. I've never seen any of you before in my life."

She shifted. "Yet we've been around."

"If that's true, then why contact me now? Huh?" I slammed my hands on the car door. "I'm not playing your game."

"I told him we should have led with the truth," she murmured.

"Him who? What truth?"

"Nuthin."

I had my suspicions, though. "Where's Jag?" Curse the irritation that blossomed because Mary watched over me and not him. Apparently, I wasn't important enough for him to watch me himself.

"Jag's busy."

"I'll bet he is. Go home, Mary. Go back to the gang and tell them to leave me alone." I slammed into my motel room, more agitated than ever. Pissed because they'd lied. Angry because I'd thought they were my friends. Hurt because it turned out that Jag had used me and wasn't really my lover. Only one person had told me the truth.

But could I believe it?

Using the motel phone, I dialed. When Braedon answered, I said in a rush, "The demon thing. I want to see proof."

31

THE GUY DIDN'T EVEN ARGUE WITH MY DEMAND.
I asked for proof, and Braedon said, "Where are you?
I'll come pick you up."

He knew the motel I named, so I had to ask,
"Hook up here often?"

"No!" he exclaimed.

"The beds are comfortable," I offered.

"Is that an invitation?"

"Maybe." Because, quite honestly, I didn't know
what I wanted. Not anymore.

Since I couldn't leave out the front door, I had to
climb out the window of my ground-floor room. I
didn't fall, which I counted as the first piece of good
luck.

I ran across the parking lot, well-lit this time of
night. The chain-link fence separating it from the

strip mall clinked as I dug my fingers and the toes of my shoes into the holes. My shirt snagged and tore going over the top, but I kept going, dropping to the ground on the other side.

I crouched, absorbing the shock. Yay, me. Then I took off running, making it around the building to the front before walking to the gas station. Five minutes later, Braedon appeared.

"You were close by," I remarked, sliding into the front seat.

"I was hungry and looking for a snack when you called." He pointed to the boxes of pizza and donuts in the back.

"Ooh. Can I?" I asked, a little more enthusiastically than warranted.

"Go ahead," he said with a chuckle. "Got a bottle of iced tea in the bag."

I half crawled into the back to drag the food onto my lap. Vending machine chips only went so far.

"I thought you were pissed at me," he admitted as he drove.

I finished my bite of cold pizza—odd if he'd just picked it up—before replying. "Not you, just life in general. It feels like it's the world against me. I'm tired of it, but at the same time, I can't keep running." Because so far, trying to escape hadn't worked. Maybe it was time I stood my ground and forced the truth. If Jag and the others were behind my problems, then I owed it to myself to find out. "Your friend agreed to meet us?"

"She did."

"Where?"

"The campus. She says that's where it all began."

What began? And why there?

We went through the college's formal front gates, more decoration than anything given that no actual fence hemmed in the campus. At this time of night, the buildings appeared dark and abandoned. To save power, only the solar lights lining the roads and paths illuminated the way.

Braedon drove us to the building with its sign repainted since my last visit. Hennessy House. Not even midnight, I'd expected it to have lights on, but only a single attic window glowed.

My room. The one that, despite Kalinda insisting we keep it, I'd not once visited.

Entering the main level, the smothering quiet proved eerie. The last few years, I'd lived in places much like Hennessy House. A few things always remained true. One, you could always expect a light on in the living room. Always. A safety thing for the students to see as they navigated the area to their dorms. Two, illuminated public areas decreased the rate of assaults.

Maybe the dark areas had to do with energy-saving? I certainly didn't sense anything nefarious lurking in the shadows, but then again, I'd recently learned that my gut instinct wasn't worth shit.

No one lay on the couch with their phone or a book. The reception desk sat empty—or so it seemed until I peeked over it and noticed someone lying on the floor asleep. So much for security.

Braedon didn't seem spooked as he unerringly headed for the stairs as if he'd been here before.

I yawned. Damn, I could have used a nap. I felt utterly drained. The couch looked tempting.

"You coming?" I realized Braedon held the door to the stairwell open, waiting for me.

I shoved past the sudden fatigue to join him. He trotted to the first landing with me on his heels. A glance down the hall showed not a single glow under any of the doors. A coldness trickled past me, making me shiver.

My eyes drooped. Weariness tugged at me. Wanted me to sit down for a moment. Rest a second. I kept moving upward, pushing past it to the floor that'd almost become my home. I had to wonder how my campus life would have progressed if I'd ignored Kalinda that day.

I couldn't believe she'd used me, too. I'd

genuinely thought she'd tucked me under her wing because she liked me.

Braedon didn't knock at the attic room's door, simply entered as if he had every right.

I hesitated. What the fuck was I doing? I could sense that something about this place was off. Something not quite right. Yet, if I left now, I'd never get any answers.

The deep breath I took sustained me as I stepped into the room and exhaled roughly as I saw my mother.

32

M𝚈 ᴍᴏᴛʜᴇʀ ᴡᴀꜱ ᴅᴇᴀᴅ. Sᴏ, ɴᴀᴛᴜʀᴀʟʟʏ, I screamed and reeled.

Braedon kept me from fleeing. "Abby!"

"Abby!" the woman parroted, mocking me. I heard it then, the wrongness of her voice.

I frowned and straightened, eyeing the doppelganger more closely. I saw the features that hadn't aged a day, the hair done differently, the makeup darker than my mom ever wore. And the clothes: tight jeans, crop top, and heels. Mom preferred comfort over style.

"Who are you?" I asked.

"Who do you think I am?" she countered.

Braedon was confused. "You're not who I'm supposed to meet. Where's Selena?"

Fake-Mom snorted. "You're in the right place,

college boy. And thank you for doing my dirty work. Braedon, you have to get Abby away from those kids. They're dangerous," she crooned.

Braedon recoiled. "Selena? How? What?"

"So pretty. So dumb," she said, getting close enough to pat his cheek. He froze as if a switch had been turned off. She eyed me next. "You, though, are plain. Boring. Blame that human whore of his. He could have had so much more had he chosen wiser." She *tsked* as she finished her strange claim. Her words made no sense.

"I don't understand."

"Of course, you don't. Because he never wanted you to know what he truly was. Would you love a demon, Abigail?" the woman coaxed.

"Demons don't exist."

"You are so wrong. And I will prove it." Fake-Mom smiled with sharp teeth and a gaze more suited to a feral animal. "Watch." She waved her hand, and an image appeared on the back of the white-painted door. Yet I'd seen no projector.

As the video played, I recognized Kalinda in the professor's kitchen, mixing away while wearing her apron, her makeup and hair perfect. Mary sat at the counter, laptop open.

I smirked. "Wow, look at those demons. Baking and working. Horrifying."

"Keep watching."

As if synchronized, both Mary's and Kalinda's heads turned at the same time. Kalinda's mouth opened, and she must have called out because the professor rushed in, followed by Cashien and Jag. Then, chaos ensued as the windows in the kitchen blew out.

I cried out even as they ducked. Still, the shards flying around like sharp bullets must have hurt. Kalinda rose first, and in my mind, I heard her melodic cursing. As I watched on the strange screen, her elegant face took on a sharper cast. Her eyes began to glow, but she didn't completely Hulk out of her clothes until the first monster came through the window.

Cat-sized, winged creatures with pointed teeth and claws poured into the professor's kitchen and attacked. My friends physically changed—not much, but enough for me to see the monsters within. Their faces took on an alien cast, their teeth became sharper, and their fingers elongated into claws. Claws that tore into flesh.

The video disappeared.

I clapped. "Nice special effects."

"You don't believe?"

"Come on. I've seen how shit can be manipulated. Of course, I don't believe it. Not when you've obviously got some kind of agenda. Getting a face mask to look like my mom. Trying to alienate me from my friends." Friends I'd ditched on the word of a guy who'd brought me to the real psycho.

"They're not your friends."

As she said it, it hit me hard that while they might have lied about some things, in all other respects, they'd been on my side. Giving me an alibi, a place to call home, protection from the shit circumstances trying to bring me down. "I'm done listening to your bullshit. Find someone else to fuck with."

"There is no one else I'd rather ruin, though," she cajoled.

It hit me then. "You're the one making those pentagrams. You killed those people."

"I did. And I'll kill many more. Including you, if I don't get what I want."

Was this about money? "Exactly what do you think I can give you? I don't have any money." Not entirely true, but I wasn't about to let her think for a second that I'd give in to blackmail.

"You think this is about money? Ha." Fake-mom snorted. "I want something more invaluable than that. Something that can't be bought."

"Get to the fucking point already." I rolled my eyes.

"Revenge," she said with a sadistic twist of her lips.

I almost wanted to clap at her performance. "Revenge for what? I've never met you before, lady."

Rather than reply, she twirled away from me. "Did you know I was once enrolled at this school? Stayed in this very room, as a matter of fact. With a woman named Lily Baker."

The name hit me like a hammer. "You knew my mom?" Not for long, obviously. Mom had told me she dropped out in the first semester.

"Oh, I knew her, all right. As if I'd forget the whore who stole my fiancé!"

33

I COULD ADMIT, I GLANCED AROUND FOR A hidden camera. This couldn't be happening. My mom? A man-stealer?

"I think you're mistaken." I remained polite in case Fake-Mom's insanity turned from irrational to violent. And what the fuck was wrong with Braedon? He hadn't said a word or even moved a muscle. If I didn't know better, I'd say he was paralyzed in place.

"No mistake. Our parents arranged it at our birth, intent on joining our two lines. It would have been a powerful union."

"So he wasn't really your fiancé," I argued. "His family was forcing him."

"It wasn't forcing. He wanted it until he met *her*," she spat.

Her obviously being my mom. "He dumped you because he fell in love."

"That human whore stole him from me. Humiliated me."

The way she said "human" had me asking, "If you're not human, then what are you?"

"Demon." Her lips curved into a cruel smile. "And so is your father."

I laughed. "My dad is not evil incarnate." I'd seen him fast-forward the beginning of certain kid movies to spare me the parent dying. He made pancakes in heart shapes.

"Your father was a highly placed demon until he left it all for *her*. And I lost everything when my brother ended up marrying a cousin from your family instead. Because of your whore mother, I became nothing."

The revenge now made so much sense, as did other things. "You're the reason we moved all the time."

Her lips curved. "Dear Geoffrey. He led me on a merry chase. But in the end, I found him. And I hurt him like he hurt me. By taking away his slut."

The breath left me in a rush that had me wavering and sightless. My lips—hell, my whole face and soul—were numb as I muttered, "You killed my parents."

"Only your mother. And not intentionally. I planned to torture her, which in turn would have plagued your father. However, the police spotted her driving the car and chased us. I barely survived the crash."

Once more, my brain took a second to catch up. "You were in the car with my mom? What about my dad?"

"That coward went deep into hiding. Once I recovered, I went looking but couldn't find him. Which is why I decided to see what would happen if I played with you. His only daughter."

I reeled from the influx of information. The threats by a psycho wanting revenge for being jilted. My dad was possibly alive but ignoring me. Leaving me alone.

Maybe he was a demon. It would explain why he didn't love me.

"My dad doesn't care about me. If he did, he would have shown himself to me by now."

"I know Geoffrey. He wouldn't abandon you. However, he would pretend to be dead if he thought it would protect you."

"Guess again. I don't know where my dad is."

"Close by, I'd wager. Probably even one of those you call friend. But which mask is he wearing? He wasn't hiding inside that kid Peter, or Jackson. Now that you're in my grasp, we'll soon find out which body he chose."

Fuck me, I was so screwed. I knew better than to expect my daddy to come riding to my rescue. "Your plan won't work. My dad's not here."

"Then I guess you'll die."

34

FAKE-MOM SNAPPED HER FINGERS, AND suddenly, Braedon could move and talk. "What the fuck, Selena? I did not bring Abby here for you to hurt her. I would never—"

"Shh." Fingers to her lips, Fake-Mom shushed him, and Braedon's lips sealed shut, as in no seam, no hole.

Holy fuck.

"What did you do?" I squeaked. "What's happening?"

"Demon magic." She winked at me. "Or did you think *demon* was just a word? Our kind is special. Able to do great things. Like silence annoying humans. Behave, or I'll do the same to you."

It was one thing to pshaw a video that could be

doctored, another for it to happen right in front of me. "Let us go. We're not the people you're mad at."

Her tinkling laughter held a discordant tone. "As if that matters. Blood is blood, and I'll need lots of it if I'm to swap this hideous face and body for something more attractive." She grimaced. "I still can't believe he chose *her* over me." She spoke of changing her face as if it were an outfit.

"I don't know how you expect to draw out my dad, hiding in this room."

"By now, he'll know you're missing and will have read the note I had delivered with my attacking imps. He'll meet us at the mausoleum where he first kissed the whore, thus betraying me." Her eyes glowed, and she practically spat as she hissed, "They both lied. For weeks. I should have known something was wrong when he didn't want to have sex. Males always want to rut. In Geoffrey's case, he rutted someone else."

"I'm sorry. That is a shit thing to do to someone." My weak, if honest, reply.

"Geoffrey was never a nice demon. It was why his defection for that human was so vile," she spat.

All this over a break-up? I clung to that rather than the rest. I had a harder time believing in demons existing than the fact that my dad might still be alive.

"Let's go." She waggled her fingers, and I wasn't in control. Like a puppet on strings, I went where she directed.

As we headed down the stairs, the urge to sleep hit once more, only to fade as we walked out the front door. It made me think of the security person napping on the floor. "What did you do to the students?"

"I put them all to sleep."

"You drugged them?"

"As if I'd do something so human. No, I used magic." She waggled her fingers.

Hard to doubt her claim. I only had to look at poor Braedon. He simmered with his mouth sealed shut.

"You're wasting your time with me," I argued. "My father isn't here."

"He is. The question is, which face is he wearing? The ones I sacrificed turned out to be wrong."

The casual way she spoke sent a chill through me. "Why do you keep calling murder 'sacrifice?'" If I was going to die, then I didn't care if I pissed her off. I wanted to at least understand why my life had gone to shit.

"Because a killing done right is full of power for our kind. Human souls, and even demon ones, power our magic. Make us strong."

"The pentagrams they've been finding...those were you. You framed my parents for murder."

She waved a hand. "They weren't all mine. Just because your father chose a mundane way of life didn't mean he completely eschewed his heritage."

What she implied... "My dad wasn't a killer."

"He was. Is. Cold-hearted and vicious, even among our kind. Until *she* poisoned him."

I wanted to poison this woman. Insane bitch— and the reason my life had gotten fucked up. If anyone deserved to die, painfully, it was Fake-Mom.

As we neared the gates to the cemetery attached to the college, the resting place of its founders, Fake-Mom clapped her hands, and motes of light rose and whirled, a beacon in the sky.

I struggled against the power sapping my will to fight. My body wouldn't cooperate, but my tongue still worked. "Aren't you worried someone will see?"

"No." She giggled. "And if they do, I'm an over-charged battery right now. So many deaths, so quickly. I can do anything." She flung out her hand, and a tree cracked and toppled.

I flinched.

She noticed. "How is it that someone weak like you was born to one as strong as him?"

That hurt. "I'm not weak."

"Says the human being led to her slaughter."

"Drop the spell on me, bitch, and I'll give you a fight." I struggled against the spell keeping my hands by my sides.

She laughed. "Do you really think a half-breed like you can defend against me?"

"Maybe she can't, but a full demon can," was the low, rumbled reply as Jag stepped into view.

35

HE'D COME TO MY RESCUE, BOTH FAMILIAR AND not. For one, this Jag had glowing eyes, a sharpness to his features, and a feral quality to his smile.

He also had no fear as Fake-Mom snapped at him. "You're not Geoffrey."

"Nope. But I am her boyfriend." He jerked a thumb at me. "And that means you can fuck right off. Leave Abby alone."

Fake mom—No. She wasn't my mom. Selena sniffed. "You're one of his soldiers, aren't you?" She prowled to his left.

"Geoffrey is dead," Jag declared.

"Lie," she hissed. "The coward is hiding from me."

Jag shook his head. "Maybe he was in the beginning, but grief got the best of him."

"More lies!" Selena roared. "Geoffrey would never be so weak."

"Love changes a person." He didn't look at me, and yet the way he shifted, stood in front of me, shielding me... Was it possible?

"Demons don't love. We fuck. We pursue power. We acquire wealth. We kill," Fake-Mom barked.

"*You* do. Those of us who want to survive in today's world know better than to be so brazen. Which is why it is my pleasure to inform you that the cabal has rendered a verdict regarding your recent actions."

What cabal? I frowned.

"I don't care what those old bastards have to say. Our laws say I may avenge my honor." Fake-Mom's chin lifted.

"Our laws also say you can't be indiscreet. And the way you've been killing students and not hiding your tracks is far from circumspect. I've been told to give you a choice. Surrender and face punishment or die."

Her lip curled. "I'll surrender when she's dead." Fake-Mom flung a hand.

One second, Jag stood before me. The next, a fist of air punched him, and I would have gotten slammed if Kalinda hadn't tackled me.

36

Hitting the ground never felt good, especially when you were the bottom of the face-meeting-cobblestone sandwich. The only thing that saved me from serious broken ribs was that Kalinda didn't weigh more than a hundred and thirty pounds soaking wet.

It still hurt when she barreled into me. Pretty sure I left some DNA on the rough ground. But it sure as hell beat getting plowed by Jag, who I'd bet was more than two hundred pounds. He'd been tossed a few feet past me, and after slamming into a solid monument—a man with a sword—lay unmoving on the ground, possibly dead. Definitely not getting up without medical intervention.

Kalinda scrambled off me, huffing, "You okay?"

"Define *okay*." I shoved to my feet. I hurt in too many places. Which oddly made it more bearable.

"You better be okay enough to run."

Run? "What about Fake-Mom and Jag?" He still hadn't twitched a single muscle, but I did see his chest rise and fall. He shimmered as if radiating something, yet I felt no heat.

With Jag out of the equation, the demon turned her gaze on us. More accurately, me.

Ever see a cartoon gulp? An exaggerated swallow of epic proportions? I experienced it. The fear hurt going down, a stark reminder of what Fake-Mom had said about me.

She'd called me a coward. She'd claimed I was weak.

That bitch. I didn't have to make her statement true.

"I am not running." Not when my mom's murderer, the reason for my hellish existence, stood right in front of me. Smug as fuck. I wanted to slap the smirk off her face. Grab hold of her hair and pull it. Drag her along the ground by that perfect haircut.

Blame my stinging skin for my testiness. It and my loose tooth—all her fault.

I could taste blood. Smell the coppery tang. A throbbing pain filled me, but I didn't understand the adrenaline coursing through me. The way my entire body vibrated.

Moving felt like tripping on acid. Things acquired a color trail, changing shape and density.

Jag pulsed a dark crimson, as did Kalinda, but Fake-Mom's aura was a sickly green. It roiled and pustulated around her.

I didn't need any lessons in magic to realize that I saw evil. Either that or I'd been drugged with some epic shit.

With a yell, I charged Fake-Mom. Not thinking. Not caring. Just knowing she was the reason for a good chunk of the bad things in my life.

To my surprise, she let me reach her. Still smirking.

I was gonna wipe it from her face.

The hand I raised to slap halted midair. Her lips moved, forming an O that she blew in my direction. Bands of nothing wrapped around me.

That didn't bode well.

"Stay away from her!" Kalinda yelled.

It made me warm inside to hear her coming to my aid. The idiot. Seriously, I should have followed Kalinda's plan to run.

"You're not in a position to make demands." Selena trailed a manicured nail across my skin.

I shivered.

"Don't make us fight." The new voice belonged to Cashien.

Huh. Another friend to my rescue.

"You can't really think to stop me. I feel your weakness from here. When was the last time you fed the magic?" Fake-Mom purred, tracing a sharp nail across my cheek to my ear.

"You've drunk too much of the magic. You're giving in to the madness." Cashien declared.

"Am I mad? Or are you just jealous of my strength? Of you all, the boy on the floor probably had the most potential. Too bad he didn't know how to use it."

"Let her go."

I could have cried hearing Mary's voice. Her, too? I'd never had a friend who would stand up for me. Now, I had four.

"You want me to let her go? Make me," Fake-Mom said smugly. "But let's make this interesting." She uttered a strange whistle, discordant and unpleasant.

At first, I couldn't grasp the strange, whispery sound, the thrashing like sheets on a line in a brisk breeze. Then I saw the oddest bird swoop down.

No. Not a bird.

I blinked.

A flying fucking monkey.

They were the same as in the video, impish creatures in shades of gray mottled with teal. Their tails
were long and barbed. Their wings created the flap-
ping snap as they attacked.

I caught sight of Mary dressed in a pale pink
tracksuit, her hair in jagged spikes. Her cheekbones
sharp. Facial expression feral.

Just before an imp hit, she pulled a knife and
attacked, slashing it across the attacking monster's
body. It squealed but continued reaching with
wicked claws. Mary sliced again and shouted a
word as her knife connected. A sigil on the blade
ignited. A pentagram that lit with blue before
fading, leaving the whole dagger glowing slightly.
The imp hit the ground just as the next monster
swooped in.

Two things saved Mary in that moment. One,
given the imps wanted to fly, they couldn't properly
swarm without impeding each other. The second
thing? Tiny but mighty, Mary could fight!

She did things *The Matrix* probably used stunt
doubles for, bending and moving in ways that defied
natural laws. She killed. Killed all the monsters. And
with each death, her blade grew brighter. When the
wave of imps stopped, Mary held that righteous
weapon in Fake-Mom's direction.

If I could have, I would have clapped. It was

epic. No special effects. No do-overs. Just pure, deadly athleticism. And Mary was my friend.

Rather than cower, Fake-Mom laughed. "Did you enjoy that pathetic snack? As if those puny souls are enough. A drop of water against my sea." Selena snapped her fingers, and a ball of fire appeared. "You'll run out of juice well before me."

"Let her go." My eyes widened as I heard Jag's voice from behind me.

He lived!

"You want the girl, then give me her father."

"My dad is dead." Something I grew less and less sure of. My world had turned upside down. I stared at the impossible. Maybe my father *was* alive.

If true, where the fuck was he? My anger had me simmering, but the bands of air held me tight.

"Geoffrey is very much alive, and he will turn himself over to me or the girl dies," Fake-Mom stated.

"Abby is not dying today. But you will if you don't surrender to the cabal." Jag boldly took a step forward, and the nail at my neck dug in, sharp enough to cut skin.

"Do you want to watch her die?"

"Do that, and you won't have the choice to surrender. Right now, you can still walk away alive," Jag said.

Fake-Mom giggled, the sound high-pitched,

amused, and insane. "You challenge me, knowing you can't think to match my power."

"Says you."

"I won't surrender."

"Then you'll die," Jag drawled. "Seems like the wrong choice. You sure you don't want to rethink that?"

"I'm not dying, either." Her frustration grew, and the pressure on me eased as she focused on Jag.

"You really are dumb. I'll bet that's why your fiancé dumped you."

I winced. Oooh. Low blow.

Fake-Mom whirled to face Jag. "He didn't dump me. A human whore seduced him."

"Exactly. A human who didn't even need magic. Did it occur to you that perhaps he genuinely liked Lily because you were annoying?" Jag shrugged. "I've only just met you and can see how you'd get on someone's nerves."

Her mouth rounded, and I snickered.

Bad move. Quick-tempered Fake-Mom only had to flick her hand, and my head rocked. Air punched. Pretty sure it hurt as much as a real fist.

Jag roared, "Don't touch her!"

"Or what?" She grabbed my hair and yanked.

Tears pricked my eyes.

The growling I heard didn't sound human at all.

Fake-Mom yanked my head around, drawing a sharp cry, all so she could point my face in Jag's direction. "You wanted proof of demons. Look at him. See what he truly is. What he hides."

I couldn't help but see. Jag looked like his evil twin brother, everything sharper and wilder. Feral and violent. His eyes glowed, but when he smirked over too-large teeth and said, "Don't worry, buttercup, I got this," I heard the Jag I knew. Still the same man, just a different face.

"Such balls. Maybe I'll cut them off and have them for dinner later." Fake-Mom licked her lips. My head went back as Selena held her knife over me. She liked her drama, and she milked it as she held the blade poised. "Give me Geoffrey, or she dies."

"You won't escape this alive. Is revenge worth it?" Cashien asked.

"So worth it. Once I kill you all, I'll be even more powerful. Maybe I'll have a talk with the cabal." She clicked her tongue. "Thinking they can dictate to me." Fake-Mom sneered. "Perhaps it's time to replace them."

"Good luck with that." Jag dropped to one knee and placed his dagger on the ground. He then touched it and mumbled a word.

"What feeble trick are you trying now?" Fake-Mom asked.

"What's it look like?" Jag stepped away from his glowing dagger.

"Stop that." Fake-Mom wagged a finger. I no longer viewed it as innocuous. Not given what I'd seen her do.

"Surrender, and this doesn't have to end with your death," Kalinda said, and Fake-Mom spun me with her in time to see Kalinda had laid a glowing weapon down, too.

They were obviously doing something big because Fake-Mom freaked. "I won't be imprisoned! Your magic, even combined, can't stop me. Now where is Geoffrey? Because I can see clearly now, none of you are him. Where is he hiding? Is he that professor you're living with? It can't be. The power signature is all wrong."

"Hand Abby over, and no one has to get hurt." Mary's turn.

Each of my friends drew Selena's attention, disrupting and distracting. Waiting for what?

"Haven't you learned yet? Hurting is the fun part." Fake-Mom cackled like a witch.

I almost giggled. Much as I hated the banter, the longer it lasted, the longer I lived. But what about when she tired of verbal sparring? While dangling in her fist, the knife remained a threat, as did the fact that I remained trussed like a turkey.

"Give up, Selena." Cashien this time.

"Never."

"You'll never win." Jag took over next.

As each of them taunted, drawing her attention, I had to wonder at the game. The glowing weapons formed four points on a lopsided square that made no sense.

Fake-Mom—Selena—seemed to think she knew what it meant. "Are you trying to contain me?" Her laughter bubbled with derision. "As if the four of you are enough."

"You're right, we need a fifth." Kalinda tapped her chin. "Abby?"

Why did she eye me? Ever had that scary dream where you're in danger and can't scream? Opening my mouth, I discovered an inability to speak. My worst nightmare coming true.

"Don't ask Abby. Even for a half-breed, she's very ungifted," Selena taunted. "Could be I've misjudged her worth. I am beginning to see why Geoffrey doesn't care for such a weak and unsightly child. Perhaps I should do him a favor and rid him of his worst shame."

The knife lifted, and this time, I knew she wouldn't be distracted.

I closed my eyes.

Waited to die. Which was when the hero I least expected spoke. "Let her go."

"Professor?" The word formed on my lips but didn't escape.

"You're not Geoffrey, your aura is wrong," Selena declared.

The professor stood, bathed in a green and taupe light, dull and boring until he snapped his fingers. A crimson glow burst free, and I gasped at the sight of it, billowing and bold.

"There you are. At last. Geoffrey." Selena smiled in triumph.

"Yes, it's me." The voice shifted. "You wanted me, I'm here, Selena. Time we settled things between us. Leave my daughter alone." Professor-Daddy flicked a glance at me and winked. "Don't worry, Abby girl, Super Dadums is here."

My eyes widened.

Daddy?

I burst into tears.

37

IT WAS STUPID TO CRY. AFTER ALL, WHAT MADE me think the professor was actually my dad? Maybe he forgot he was supposed to be my uncle.

He glanced at me, and in that gaze, I knew. My dad suddenly reappeared from the dead, wearing my professor's body. I tried not to think of *Men in Black* and the Edgar suit.

If it was him, then why now? Why not years ago when my life went down the toilet?

Selena clapped. "Excellent disguise. I couldn't suss you out at all."

Could she see the colors, too? How did she not notice hers?

"I had time to perfect the spell." The professor— aka Fake-Uncle and now Wrong-Faced-Daddy—

kept moving, past Jag, then past Kalinda. As he moved, Selena spun me with her.

"You led me on a merry chase, Geoffrey. After Oklahoma, I almost lost faith. In the end, I didn't find you, I found the whore on the internet."

"Lily wasn't on social media," my professor-daddy declared.

"But her child was." Selena sneered at me. "I'm surprised you let her post."

"She wasn't supposed to," was the professor's snooty reply.

Or so I chose to hear it, because I couldn't deal with a disappointed father. Could this all really be my fault? If I'd not gone through that selfie phase, would Selena have never found us?

"Tell me, how many times did I get close before our final encounter?"

"A few times," he grudgingly admitted.

"Was that you in Sacramento a dozen or so years ago?"

"Yes," he hissed.

Selena smiled. "Did you like the present I left in that church?"

If I recalled correctly from my study of the crimes, they'd found a pentagram etched on the altar, the white cloth soaked in blood.

EVE LANGLAIS

"You're out of control and need to be reined in," Professor-Daddy declared. "You don't have to die."

The threat tilted Selena's lips. "Kill me, and my family would be most put out."

"With the evidence presented to the cabal, your family has already disowned you."

"Another thing that is your fault." Selena paced angrily, dragging my bobbing body behind.

"You could have been mature and just let me go." Professor-Daddy stopped partway between Mary and Cashien. Odd until he held out his hand, and it began to glow, pulling at the beams of light projecting from the weapons.

Selena lost her shit. "Don't you dare try to contain me!"

"Let my daughter go."

"Drop the containment field or I'll kill her." The knife she'd pulled pressed against my neck, pricked. I bled.

"Last warning. Let her go, Selena."

"I think not. Enjoy watching your daughter die." The blade dug deeper into my flesh, and I waited for the slash.

Only to hear a loud pop.

Suddenly, Selena acquired a red third eye.

38

WHO KNEW? A BULLET BETWEEN THE EYES could kill a demon. Also good to know was the fact that spells died with their creator.

As Selena dropped, so did I. Lucky me, I landed beside Selena's face. Her surprised expression stared at me. Her mouth was open as if to exclaim, only she'd never breathe again.

I'd come close to death before in the lab. Refrigerated or defrosting specimens. Nothing like a real and fresh corpse eyeing you accusatorily. You or me, bitch. Glad it was you.

There was a commotion.

"Who shot her?"

"Hey, it's that guy who's been hanging around Abby."

"Cashien and Jag, with me. Let's see what Braedon knows," Professor-Daddy said.

But Jag declined. "I gotta check on Abby."

Recovered from my ignoble fall, I pushed to my feet. I felt the edge of the knife that'd almost killed me and gripped it. It tingled in my grasp, and the stings in my palms—rudely abused for a second time tonight—stopped hurting. As I turned to see my friends approaching, my blade hummed, and I'd have sworn it shouted, *"Hungry!"*

You are not eating my friends. I tucked it into my pants before eyeing Kalinda and Mary, who converged on me with Jag. They didn't look like demons.

"Why are you eyeing me like that?" Kalinda snorted. "Did I get a smudge on my face? Is my hair messed up?" She reached to stroke it.

"You're a demon." Felt like I should get that point out of the way.

"And?" Kalinda rolled her shoulders.

"Doesn't that make you evil?"

"Do I look evil?" she asked, batting the lashes I envied.

"Not anymore, you don't. But earlier, you were scary as fuck." It was an honest admission, to which Kalinda laughed.

"Always remember, evil depends on what side

you're on." Mary's sage offering.

"I don't think there was a side where Selena wasn't evil." Kalinda grimaced at the body.

"This needs to be removed before the sleepy spell on campus lifts." Jag toed the body, and I winced.

"Don't look at me." Kalinda lifted her chin. "I just had my nails done."

Mary almost appeared to shrink as she gave her excuse. "My chiro says I should avoid heavy lifting."

Jag huffed. "For fuck's sake." He whistled. "Cash, I need a hand."

Cashien jogged over and didn't ask questions. Apparently, they did this kind of thing often given how seamlessly they set into motion the cleaning of the crime scene.

Cashien and Jag carried off the body while Kalinda and Mary scrubbed, Mary moving her hands in a way that pulled water from the nearby pond and washed the floor. Kalinda went around zapping the security cameras that had documented our actions, frying the systems. Mary would wipe any additional records clean as soon as they finished here.

I felt useless and in the way as they worked, but I remained watching, avoiding the professor and Braedon, who still held his smoking gun. Surely, I'd been mistaken about the professor being my daddy. He'd probably spoken that way to lull Selena into a false sense of security.

I had to find out for sure. Reluctantly, I moved in their direction.

"That was quite the act you pulled." My weak attempt to find out the truth without sounding crazy.

The prof's lips turned down. "I think you know by now that wasn't an act, Abby girl."

"You expect me to believe you're my father?"

He nodded.

"How?"

"That's vague as questions go, but if you mean the face,"—he rubbed his jaw—"I used the same kind of magic Selena employed to change her appearance."

"Demon magic that needs a sacrifice."

It took him a second before he nodded sharply. "Killing to absorb the power of death is what our kind does. It strengthens us. But at the same time, we have to temper our impulses because too much death drives you mad. Like Selena."

It explained a little but not the thing I wanted to know most. "Why did you abandon me?"

For a second, his mouth worked. "Because I was dumb."

The worst and best answer he could have given.

When I didn't reply, he spread his hands.

"When Selena framed your mother and me, we had to go. We meant to return for you when things died down, only I went out for supplies one day, and Selena caught your mother. Next thing I knew, the papers had us listed as dead. I thought..."—he paused —"I thought if I went along with it, you'd have a chance for a normal life. A safe one."

"The media named me Slaughter Daughter."

"I know."

"It followed me everywhere. Ruined my life. Made me a pariah. You left me alone." The betrayal burned.

He rolled his shoulders. "And for that, I'm sorry. I know I can't erase what happened, but I'm here now. If you'll give me another chance."

I wanted to say no. To tell him to go to Hell. But even in another body, it was still my dad. "Fine, but I don't suppose you can change into something a bit uglier. Because I want to gag now that I thought of you for even a second as the hot professor."

His lips twisted. "I can see that might be a problem. How about I return to the face you know already?"

My expression lightened. "Can you?" Only to grimace as I said, "Will you have to kill someone?"

He hesitated before nodding.

Did it matter that much? "Can you at least make

sure it's a bad guy?" Then it could be considered a civic duty.

He grinned. "I smell a Marvel marathon coming on."

"No." I groaned. At last count, there were over thirty hours of it. His offer just further proved the impossible. My dad was alive.

And a demon.

"Shall we go home?" he asked.

"Wasn't it attacked by flying monkeys?"

He grimaced. "Don't remind me. The kitchen is a mess, but the rest of the house is fine."

"Okay."

"Okay?" Braedon, silent until now, blurted, "You can't go anywhere with him. Professor Santino just admitted he's a demon who kills people. They all do."

"It's not ideal," I admitted with a shrug. Perhaps my study of death had made me more nonchalant in the face of it. The planet did have issues with over-crowding, and some people were a waste of space.

"Not ideal?" Braedon exclaimed. "They're murderers. Selena lied to me. She told me demons were just like us, but with magic. She never said that magic came at the cost of someone's life."

"Is that really how it works?" I asked my dad, knowing the answer but wanting confirmation.

He glanced at Braedon and nodded. "The spark that inhabits living flesh is power, all death feeds the magic, with humans offering the strongest boost."

"You killed before arriving. That's why they were stalling," I surmised.

Professor-Daddy nodded. "I didn't want to be weak when facing her. I have much to tell you, but we should move. This location has to be scrubbed." He then glanced at Braedon. "Remember what I told you."

"I remember. If I talk, I'll die, too," he said sullenly.

"Don't forget it." Then the professor eyed me. "Let's go, Abby."

Braedon stepped between us. "Don't, Abby. I know you're not okay with this."

"Leave her alone." Professor-Daddy intervened, but this was one battle I didn't need help with.

"I'm fine. Let me talk with Braedon for a minute. Go to the car. I assume it's parked by the dorm. I'll meet you there in a minute."

I waited until my dad was out of earshot before starting. "Listen, Braedon—"

He didn't listen. He grabbed me and kissed me thoroughly.

And then he wasn't anymore as Jag tore him from me, roaring, "Get the fuck away from her."

"Or what? You'll kill me? Look at him, Abby." Braedon pointed. "See what he is. Is that really what you want?

Jag's shoulders rounded, and his features lost some of their sharpness.

"Walk away from him," Braedon urged, holding his gun on Jag. "I'll keep you safe. Together, we'll make sure these demons don't kill any more."

"How?" I asked.

"By exposing them to the world."

"You can't do that," Jag growled. "You'll kill us all."

"Exactly. Maybe I'll start with you. After all, I'll need proof." Braedon smirked and I knew in that moment he'd actually shoot Jag.

"Don't." I stepped between them. "You'll make a mess, and people might not understand."

"Is that the reason, or do you still care for him?" Braedon asked, the gun waving around.

"If I cared for him, would I be leaving with you?" I said as I walked to Braedon. I could feel Jag's hurt. Saw Braedon's triumph.

The golden human versus the dark demon.

The choice had never been clearer. I reached Braedon and hugged him, whispering, "I'm sorry." Because he'd forgotten one crucial thing.

I was half-demon, and I had a knife.

39

H‍AVING SPENT YEARS STUDYING DEATH, I KNEW how to cut in a way that took Braedon out and didn't make him suffer. I didn't have a choice. I already knew he was dead. The way they cleaned that crime scene, the secret they had to keep? They weren't about to let a non-demon, a human, destroy them.

Braedon had to go. It seemed only right that I take him out since I had drawn him into this mess.

The body hadn't even hit the floor when I felt myself lifted and spun in Jag's arms. He crushed his mouth to mine. Fiercely. Possessively.

"Are you okay? You didn't have to do that. I would have handled him," Jag exclaimed.

Yes, he would have, and he would always have wondered where my loyalty lay. I was a half-demon in love with a demon. It explained my fascination with death. And now that I'd finally killed, I could feel it inside me, coursing through my veins: power and ecstasy.

It bubbled up in me, escaping as laughter. "What's happening to me?" I asked.

"Magic, buttercup. It would seem you're more demon than anyone knew."

And then his mouth was back on mine. But not for long as Kalinda returned, hissing and cursing melodically. "Would you two save it for later? We need to get out of here. Cashien's coming back for the body."

That of the man I'd killed. I shoved aside the guilt as I ran off with my demon lover.

As we sat in the back seat—meaning the terrifying Kalinda was behind the wheel of her Jeep—I couldn't help but worry. "The campus cameras will have caught everything. I'm going to jail."

Look at my cold ass, worried about being arrested and not the man now dead by my hand.

Jag's palm came to rest on my thigh. He squeezed my leg and, that easily, I knew I would do it again. He leaned close. "Don't worry. Cashien and the others will fix it."

"How can I help?"

Apparently, by staying out of the way and being sent to bed with Jag just in case I needed an alibi.

Entering my room, I began to pace. "This is bad."

"We're fine." Jag flopped on the mattress, hands tucked behind his head.

"We are not fine."

"I know something that will make you feel better." He winked and patted the comforter.

I made a face. "Really?"

He just nodded. Slowly. And then smiled. When he peeled off his shirt, I lost the battle.

I joined him, partially undressed but with his hands skimming over flesh. Soon, we were skin to skin.

We kissed. Hungry. Needy.

I clung to him as he sank into me, gasped as he filled me perfectly. I rode him, undulating against him as he thrust into me, our lips meshed, along with our hearts and breaths.

When I came, I let myself be swept away, up and out of my body, to a place where hot and cold became one.

My naked limbs twined with his, the glow of sex still surrounding me, I trailed my fingers over his chest. "What's next? Shouldn't we be packing?"

"I'd rather sleep with you. Let's figure shit out in the morning."

When I proved a little too energetic for slumber,

he made love to me a second time. Then a third, until I finally drowsed beside him.

By the time I woke the next day, the front page of the paper had the story. And it was a good one.

Copycat Killer Taken Out by Her Victim.

It appeared an unidentified woman had been found, dead of a bullet wound to the head. The police claimed that her death was a last-ditch effort escape by the man she'd sacrificed. He'd pulled a gun and shot her moments before dying in the pentagram she'd drawn.

In a shocking twist, DNA evidence tied her to a few more crime scenes across the country. The Pentagram Killer had been caught. My parents' names were cleared, along with mine.

I was finally free.

EPILOGUE

GIVEN THAT I NO LONGER HAD AN AX HANGING over my head, nor any interest in following a mundane career, I dropped out of school and relocated to Europe with the gang.

We took up residence in a veritable castle. Me, my demon lover, and my demonic friends. Daddy, no longer the professor, reclaimed his old face, minus a few wrinkles. We'd finally hugged, cried, and talked before crying some more as we reminisced about my mom.

At times, I tried to guilt him over leaving me, but Daddy remained steadfast. "I did it to protect you because I knew you were better off without me."

"I wasn't," I pouted. But it was hard to stay mad. After all, in the end, I'd gotten everything I ever wanted, including a heritage I'd never expected. I

EVE LANGLAIS

learned everything I could about being a demon. Turned out, some half-breeds could use blood magic.

And use it I did. It turned out my guilt diminished the more I killed. My first taste of blood was the catalyst to me becoming my father's slaughter daughter. Magic was addictive. But lucky for me, human souls deserving of death were plentiful.

With my new hobby making me seek out bad guys, it occurred that maybe I needed a new name. One more suited to my unique and distinct identity. Slaughter Witch? Nah. Bitch on a Broom?

Ha.

"What's so funny?" Jag asked, brushing a hand over my naked thigh.

"Just imagining myself as a robed crusader with a pointy hat, riding a broom, ridding the city of criminals."

"Make it a short skirt with no panties, and I can give you a better ride than a broom."

"Oh, really? Prove it."

He did, but not in bed as expected. The convertible he showed me in the garage was sexy. The wanna-be rapist we killed together an aphrodisiac. The pentagram we drew gave me the adjustments to my face and body I'd always wanted.

The next morning, the local papers made us famous.

"The Satanic Butcher?" I yelled. "Did they not translate the signature I left behind?"

Apparently, I'd need to hire a press secretary if I were to get any social media love. Or I could ask Mary for a favor.

Working her keyboard magic, Mary fixed my vigilante title to *The Witch*. Simple and classic.

Paired with a short skirt and bitching thigh-high boots, my crime-fighting career was born.

THE END

OR SHOULD ABBY EMBARK ON A CRIME FIGHTING CAREER WITH HER

DEMON LOVER? THAT DEPENDS ON YOU.

For more books, visit EveLanglais.com